THE FAI

Final exams are always an ordeal for the nurses at
Middleton Royal, and for Annabel Lake exam tension is not helped by her unhappy love life. Antag-
onising the new surgeon Simon Dell just about
confirms her uncertain future.

THE FAITHFUL FAILURE

BY
KATE NORWAY

MILLS & BOON LIMITED
London · Sydney · Toronto

First published in Great Britain 1968
by Mills & Boon Limited, 15–16 Brook's Mews,
London W1A 1DR

This edition 1984
© Kate Norway 1968

Australian copyright 1984
Philippine copyright 1984

ISBN 0 263 74545 7

Set in 11 on 12 pt Linotron Times
03/0184

Photoset by Rowland Phototypesetting Ltd
Bury St Edmunds, Suffolk
Made and printed in Great Britain by
Richard Clay (The Chaucer Press) Ltd
Bungay, Suffolk

For Sandra White

CHAPTER ONE

AT Middleton Royal we took our hospital finals at the end of the third-year study block. They were reputed to be more difficult than the State finals which came a few weeks later, but several people had been known to sail through the hospital exams and flop hopelessly in the State; and one way and another we were all pretty apprehensive in my set, like other sets before us.

The evening before the first of the hospital papers—it was to be Paediatrics—Triss McDonough and I sat on Molly Leonard's bed, flapping a bit. 'We three may be split up after this,' Molly said in a worried little voice. 'There's no guarantee that we'll all get through together. The last lot had forty per cent failures, remember.'

'No, that was the State,' Triss reminded her. 'All but one were through the hospital's, for once. Only Rachel Cowie had to take it again. So much for the theory that the State's easier than the hospital thing.'

'Oh, I don't think the State *papers* are as bad as ours', I said. 'But the practical can be pretty fierce. They seem to have such a niggly pack of examiners—remember that ghastly type last year who reduced Mary Hunt to tears?—and if you're in a strange hospital, using strange gear, it can be rough.'

'Then thank God the Royal's an exam centre. At least we'll be on our own ground, using our own equipment. The girls who come here from the General for the State'll be properly flummoxed. Do you know, they don't use *any* disposables at all, over there! They'll be lost when it comes to laying up trolleys and things.'

'Oh, the General,' I said disparagingly. 'What do you expect? It's run by fuddyduddies.' And even Molly murmured: 'They don't seem very up-to-date, do they?'

There was a kind of good-natured feud between us at the Royal and the girls at the old General, the other side of town. Once we'd both been independent voluntary hospitals, until authority had seen fit to knock us all into one group, together with the Maternity Hospital, the Children's and Candley Hall mental hospital. We considered the General old-fashioned and drab. The General girls thought the Royal was snobbish. We usually managed to hang on to the inter-hospitals tennis and swimming cups. Their matron didn't encourage sport. Yet it was quite obvious that we nearly always had better exam results than they did, in spite of 'wasting time playing games'. We put this down to the fact that our young Principal Tutor was a good deal more progressive than old Miss Crump at the General, who had persisted from the steam-kettle era. Miss Black was all for wearing mufti in the schoolroom, and driving us out to see life in the evenings when we were in study-block. Miss Crump went on like some sort of purdah supervisor, and frowned on outings, boy-friends, jeans and make up as works of the devil that no Nice Girl would wish to know anything about.

I looked down at the notebook in my hand. 'I thought we were supposed to be going over our Paediatrics notes tonight?'

'No.' Triss reached out with her big square hand and snapped the book shut. 'What we don't know now, we never shall. Anyhow, Abby, you'll be all right. You've spent longer at the Kids' than any of us. You've had more than two changes there, surely?'

'Worse luck,' I said. 'I landed for that wretched Salisbury woman both times. I'm sure she's crazy.'

Triss grinned. 'I know. She won't let you boil bottles and teats—they've got to go into this fancy solution of hers for about an hour, so if you drop one everything's got to wait while—'

Home Sister stuck her head round the door. 'It *is* well after eleven,' she mentioned. 'And you do have an exam tomorrow. I know you third-years don't have an official lights-out, but do be sensible.'

I got up from Molly's bed and collected my sponge-bag, towel and notebook. 'Just breaking it up, Miss Appleby.'

'Paediatrics tomorrow, is it?'

I nodded. 'Yes. We don't know a thing!'

'Rubbish,' she said. 'It's largely common sense. And the paper's set by Dr Machin, and I'm sure *he's* a generous marker.'

'He'll need to be,' Molly told her. 'Honestly, all I can remember is pyloric stenosis, congenital hearts and chorea.'

'Then let's hope those are the compulsory questions . . . Come along, Nurse Lake, Nurse McDonough. I want to go to bed if you don't, and I've a few more little commiseration meetings to read the Riot Act to yet.'

I said goodnight to the others and walked along the corridor with Home Sister. When we got to my room she said: 'Well, good luck, Nurse. Miss Black's expecting this year's medallist to emerge from your set, you know, so do your best. After all, if you know your work—and you should after three years—you ought to be able to answer a few simple questions on it.'

'Simple!' I said. 'Miss Appleby, did you *see* the last lot of papers? They couldn't have been worse if we'd been fifth-year medical students.'

She sighed. 'I know. It *is* all getting more difficult. We've just got to make it tougher for the registration people and milk off some good people into the Enrolled stream. Things are all getting so technical nowadays—we can't afford not to have the very best, academically, as SRNs. You'll all have to specialise more in future, too . . . What do *you* want to do when you finish, Nurse?'

I thought about Tom Fitzgibbon and said: 'I don't really know. It depends . . . Maybe I'll go to America for a year and earn some real money before I decide.'

'What about midwifery?'

'There's no point. I'd never use it. If I have a ward one day I'd like men's surgical.'

'And then?'

I frowned. 'How do you mean, Miss Appleby?'

'When you've been a ward sister for a couple of years, why not go on and do Tutorial?'

'What, *me*?' I was amused. 'I wouldn't have the brains.' Nor, I thought, did I want to contemplate staying on long enough to become a Tutor; though of course if one did marry the hours were rather useful.

'Think about it,' she advised me. 'We're going to need a great many more qualified Tutors.'

'Yes,' I said. 'I'll think about it.'

But when I got into bed and put out the light at last, I didn't think about the future in those terms at all. As far as I was concerned it all hung on Tom. He had been Sir Henry's registrar for a fair time, and now that his chief was retiring he had a very good chance of a consultancy. And if he got it, then a great many things we had never openly discussed might come to fruition. If he didn't, he was likely to leave Middleton altogether. Either way, I wasn't at all sure where I stood, because Tom wasn't the kind to tie himself down until he was good and ready. And although he'd taken me about fairly steadily for the last twelve months, and for six of them had done so exclusively, he had never said anything very definite about marriage—except that he thought it improvident to launch out on a resident's salary.

Triss had always declared that Tom wasn't the

marrying kind, but then Triss had Alan's engage-
ment ring safely round her neck on a bit of bandage, and they meant to marry as soon as he could
get a GP partnership, once she was State Registered.

Molly had different ideas. She was the most
dedicated of all of us, and I could guess exactly
what she would be doing in ten years' time—
precisely what she was doing now, only she'd be
doing it in a navy blue dress and a frilly cap. She was
a very good nurse, and that said it all. I don't think
she had ever been out with the men, except when
Triss and I had dragged her off to parties. The
assistant biochemist had once been interested, but
Molly wasn't the possessive kind, and one of the
physiotherapists had whipped him from under her
nose before he even got round to asking for a date.
Molly didn't seem to mind much. She'd wanted to
be a nurse ever since she was a little girl, and that
was all she asked of life. It was simple for her.

It was simple for Triss too. She had her future all
planned out. All she wanted was to be 'Dr Longmore's wife'. But for me there was a two-way tug. I
loved my job, and I couldn't imagine ever wanting
to do anything else—I was downright sorry for girls
who had to work in shops and offices, or on the
stage, or as models—but I did want to have a home
of my own as well, and children of my own, instead
of a hospital bedroom and other people's babies. I
wanted normal children, not the kind I'd seen in
Sister Salisbury's ward—sick children, children
with malformations, children who'd been neg-

lected or ill-treated and some who would have done better not to be born at all. Tom's children, perhaps. Tall and fair and laughing, and bursting with health, like him. Maybe just one daughter who was small and dark like me, to be spoiled by her brothers. I was pretty sure that these were the things I really wanted, ultimately, but I was not in the least optimistic about getting them. Meanwhile I was happy simply doing the things I'd been trained to do.

Miss Black read out the questions to us before we began the paper, next day, and then she grinned and said: 'Good luck, Nurses!' before she left us. Miss Crisp and Mrs Inge, her assistants, stayed to invigilate.

It wasn't such a bad paper, after all. One of the compulsory questions was on phenylketonuria, and I really went to town on that, because Alan Longmore's chief, Dr Bracebridge, was an authority on it, and Alan had passed on a lot of stuff to Triss and me when they'd had a case over at the Children's and he'd been to see it. I was well up on acrodynia too, and I put quite a lot into a question about cleft-palate surgery. The ones on congenital hip dislocation, and rheumatic carditis, were easy. We had a post-mortem on it after lunch, and most of our set—there were twenty of us—seemed relieved. Molly was anxious about the surgery bits, because she'd tackled a question about intus-susception and she'd never actually seen the op. But when she found out that most of the others hadn't, either, she calmed down. 'At any rate,' I told her, 'if there are marks for tidiness you'll come top, hands down. I wish I could be as neat as you are. I never could write decently—I'm always in too much of a hurry.'

'You're telling me!' Triss said. 'I had to read a report of yours once, and I've never seen such abominable scribble in my life. Exactly as if a spider with talipes had limped out of the inkpot.'

I sighed. 'I can't help it. My brain goes faster than my pen and I can't catch up somehow . . . Well, if the Medicine paper's no worse than that we shan't do so badly, shall we?'

'Remember who's setting it,' Triss warned us. 'Dr Fussy Farnes. Now last year, when it was Dr Bracebridge, it was jammy. But Farnes is so brilliant that he expects everyone else to be the same. I must get Alan to prime me a bit tonight . . . I suppose you'll be seeing Tom, will you?'

I still didn't know. Normally, if I'd been on a ward, he would have rung me. But when we were in study-block it wasn't quite so simple. The only telephone in the nursing school was in Miss Black's office, and we were only over in the Home in the evenings, so I was feeling rather out of touch. 'I expect so,' I said. 'It's Tuesday. It's supposed to be his half-day, and he knows I'm free too, so . . .'

He didn't ring the dining-room during lunch, though one of the domestics fetched Triss to take a call from Alan, and one or two others had calls. Then I remembered that it was list-day for Wards 3 and 4. He was probably still in theatre. It was a silly day to choose for a half-day, but he had done it originally to fit in with me, when I was on the geriatric unit.

When I went over to the Home I waited until a giggling first-year came out of the booth, and then I got through to the switchboard and asked: 'Can you get Mr Fitzgibbon, please?'

Mrs Keatley was on duty. She was all right. She said: 'That you, Nurse Lake? Oh, I've a message for you. Mr Fitz is still in theatre, and he says he'll be tied up till teatime, but he'll pick you up at six if that's OK.'

'That'll be fine,' I said. 'Will you tell him?'

'If he doesn't call me, I'll bleep him later, yes.'

'Thanks,' I said. 'You're a pet. Your sparring partner wouldn't do as much.'

'Who—Miss Wallace? Oh, *well* . . . she was brought up to believe that nurses shouldn't frat with residents. She was here in Matron Smythe's day, remember. They must have had a dull life in those days, mustn't they, dear?'

'They must,' I agreed. '*If* they obeyed the rules.' Then I put the receiver down, reflecting that Molly Leonard would really have fitted in better in the old days. Men were just a distraction as far as she was concerned. I envied her such detachment, but at the same time I couldn't see much pleasure in a life without Tom or someone like him. And whatever the old guard might tell us, I didn't believe that Florence Nightingale had ever advocated spinster-hood. In fact, according to Miss Black, she had stated categorically that she was not trying to found a religious order, but a well-paid profession for women. She certainly did plenty of fratting herself. She had to.

Tom's Mini was outside the Home at precisely six o'clock. I didn't go out until I could see it from my bedroom window, and by the time I got downstairs and into the forecourt he was out of the car, leaning on its roof, and talking sixteen to the dozen to Sister Pleydell, who had just come off duty, huddled into her cape. It was nearly dark, and the porch-light made her fair hair look like tinsel. I hung back until she left him. 'Far be it for me to interrupt your little *tête-à-tête* with Theatre Sister,' I said as I climbed into the car. 'Not that I blame you—she's a very attractive young woman, from what I can see.'

Tom looked surprised. 'Is she? I hadn't noticed. We were talking about a case we had this afternoon, actually.' He shoved the gear lever over and we shot down the drive and round the bend by the mortuary. 'It was a choledochotomy. Of course, Sir Henry always used to do a cholecystectomy for common bile duct bung-ups, but this chap Dell . . .'

He went on about Mr Dell, who was filling in for Sir Henry until they sorted out the new appointment, all the way into town, until I was frankly bored. When he parked the car at the Indian restaurant, where we usually ate, I said: 'Don't you want to know how I got on with the exam today?'

'Exam?' He brought himself back from the

theatre with difficulty. 'Lord, yes, of course. How *did* it go?'

'Not bad,' I told him. 'It was Paediatrics. Quite a decent paper, really. Medicine tomorrow—that may be tough.' I walked beside him into the restaurant and waited until he found a table, and then I went on: 'Dr Farnes is setting it this time. Well, he did the lectures, so I suppose he'll set the paper. He's right above my head half the time.'

'He's a bright chap,' Tom admitted. 'And so is Dell. What shall we have—the Ceylon curry, super-hot?'

When we had ordered he got back into his mask and gown again. We went through pretty well the entire day's theatre list, in detail, while we ate. Or at least, Tom did. In the end I said: 'Tom, don't you *ever* think about anything but shop? Not even on your half-day?'

'Sorry.' He smiled at me across the table, and his eyes were very blue in the light from the little brass lamp between us. 'I do go on a bit, don't I? But this fellow has quite a few—Oh, there I go again! What *shall* we talk about?'

'How about this do the residents are having on Saturday evening, then?'

'Oh, yes. There's that.' He didn't sound in the least enthusiastic. 'Do you want to come?'

'Is that an invitation?'

'Well, of course. It won't be all that gay, though. It's only a farewell for Maggie Root. She's off on Sunday.'

'So we'll be having a new HS, as well as a new

consultant? Who'll we get, do you know?'

'One of the new batch just down, I dare say. Unless young Heathcote comes over from Cas. He's all right. I dare say he's trainable.'

'Isn't he the one with the Triss-type hair?'

'Carroty, yes.' He looked me over. 'That hair of Triss's is dreadful. She'd be quite good-looking if she had something more like yours, that sort of—'

'Rich mouse?'

'Nothing like it. It's a—a nice dark brown. The sort of hair-colour that hair ought to be.'

'Thanks,' I said. 'If it was meant as a compliment.'

'I like your hair. It's always so shiny.'

I liked his too, but I didn't say so. 'That's because I use the right shampoo. I must be TV-conscious or something.'

'Are you? I always thought you were independent, Abby. A girl with a mind of her own.'

'I'm not a careerist, if that's what you mean?' I told him. The last thing I wanted was for Tom to see me as a committed Molly Leonard. 'Once I'm an SRN I shall relax. I'm not mad keen to press on towards matronhood—not the hospital kind, anyway.'

Tom was amused. 'You'd make a jolly good matron. I can just see you laying down the law.'

'I'm not like that at all!' I protested. 'I'm not at all bossy!'

'No, love.' He put his hand over mine on the table. 'I was only ribbing.' There was a faint frown between his eyes.

His warm touch had its usual effect, and I felt I'd been irritable. 'Oh, Tom, I don't mean to be edgy, it's just that the exams are a bother. We're all in a bit of a stew.'

'Of course . . . I'm in one myself, as a matter of fact, over this consultancy business.'

'You've a good chance, surely? You did get your Fellowship first go, and that's more than a lot of people can say. It ought to count for something, oughtn't it?'

'Yes. But so did the other chaps. There's fierce competition. I'm afraid.'

'When will you know?'

'Beginning of the week, maybe. Wish me luck?'

'You know I do, Tom. If you do get it—' I left it at that.

'I probably won't. In that case I shall move on, I think.'

'Where?'

'London, perhaps. Or perhaps I'll join the brain-drain. Get a bit of lolly at the back of me.'

'I shall miss you if you go,' I said. 'Dreadfully.'

That got me precisely nowhere, because he began to talk about a man named Fowkes, who'd recently left the General, and who'd landed a job at three times the pay as anaesthetist in some Texas hospital. He was still talking when the waiter came to call him to the telephone.

When he came back he said: 'Sorry, Abby, I'll have to go. Maggie's worried about the chole-dochotomy man. I'll drop you at the Home first.'

He did kiss me before I got out of the car, but his

mind wasn't on it. He was already up in Ward 3 with
Maggie Root and Night Sister. I was used to that
kind of thing, but being used to it didn't make it any
easier to bear. '*I'm* here,' I reminded him.

'I know, love.' He kissed me again quickly.
'Sorry, I've got a one-track mind. You'll just have
to put up with it tonight. I've a lot on my plate.'

I was beginning to realise that he always had.

Alan and Triss were just saying goodnight in the
Home porch as I walked up the drive. From what I
could see of them Alan was making a far better job
of it than Tom had done. On the way upstairs Triss
said: 'So you've had the same lecture too? Early to
bed and so on?'

'No. Tom was called back to a man in Three.
Maggie Root was windy or something . . . Talking
of Maggie, are you two going to her send-off on
Saturday?'

Triss looked doubtful. 'I'll go if you do. I'm not
going to be the only third-year there among a pack
of sisters, that's for sure.'

'Why not? You're entitled to go. You're engaged
to Alan.'

'Well? You're as good as engaged to Tom.
Aren't you? Or aren't you?'

'Am I?'

She stood stock still on the landing and turned
to face me. 'You haven't been squabbling, have
you?'

'No, of course not. But it's being borne in on me
more and more that Tom's not really interested in
anything but his own career. He wasn't terribly

eager to go to Maggie's party either. All he could talk about was today's list.'

'Heavens, Abby! Be reasonable! He's got to unwind to *somebody*. Alan's just the same. More than half his talk's shop. I wouldn't have much respect for him if it wasn't, to be honest. Doctors who are bored are rotten doctors, in my experience. Where's your sense of proportion? It's not like you to talk such rot.' Triss's nice round face was screwed up with anxiety. 'You do feel all right, don't you? Or is the Medicine paper hanging over you?'

'I expect that's what it is,' I agreed. 'I'll be glad when the study-block's over and we can get back to some real work. Being off the wards doesn't suit me one bit.'

'Tomorrow we shall know where we're going. They owe me a fortnight in theatre, so maybe I'll get it in now. I'm keeping my fingers crossed to get it in before the State.'

That reminded me of Sister Pleydell. I had never worked with her—she was a recent import—and I didn't think Triss had either. 'I wonder what Playdell's like?'

'No idea. Con Riley says she's smashing, but then he's a man. She's certainly easy to look at, I'll say that for her.'

As I walked along to my room I caught myself wondering what Tom thought of her. He had been working with her all day, yet he had still had plenty to say to her when she came off duty. And then I told myself not to be so idiotically jealous.

In the morning there was an interim change list up in the dining-room, mostly dealing with the redeployment of the exam set. We clustered round the notice-board after breakfast, before going over to the school. Triss had mixed feelings when she found her name. She wasn't down for theatre—Molly was going there instead—but for Ward 8, and that meant working with Alan. I was in a similar position: Ward 3 meant Tom. I'd half expected it: I hadn't worked there for some time, and I was quite happy to go back. I got on like a house on fire with Staff Hasan, and Sister Knight was pretty harmless. She didn't put on any act with those of us who remembered her as Staff Knight of Casualty.

There was a good deal of sighing as we settled down to the Medicine paper at half-past nine. It was a wicked one. Only Molly wrote steadily right through. I was one of those who had to scamper at the last minute before Miss Crisp collected the papers. Triss seemed to have finished about five minutes earlier. Maybe that was due to listening to all Alan's shop talk and in that case I might come into my own next day with the surgery paper.

'It was really quite a nice paper,' Molly said at lunch-time. 'Didn't you think so?'

I said I'd almost certainly failed. 'Still, I didn't do so badly on that bit about Simmonds' disease,' I added. 'I remembered quite a lot about it, because we had one not so long ago. Mrs Cheshire, wasn't it, Triss?'

Triss hadn't been listening, but she did now. 'Mrs

Cheshire? You mean that Addison's we had up in Two?'

I felt cold all over. 'Addison's?' I said. 'Oh, *no*!'

Triss sighed. 'What have you done now?'

'Mixed it up with Simmonds'.' I could have wept.

'You chump!'

'I don't know *what* made me do it,' I said despairingly. 'I just can't be right in the head. Why, I remember her having Addisonian crises, and everything. I must be potty!'

Triss and Molly both commiserated with me, but it didn't help a bit. Not with Finnicky Farnes marking the papers. I had been a complete idiot. It wasn't that I didn't know the work—I did. I'd simply not been concentrating properly. I could only hope that I had every one of the other questions absolutely right and might yet be saved. It didn't bear thinking about, and so that I shouldn't be tempted I dragged Molly off to the local cinema. I didn't think about exams, or Tom, or anything else for hours. Not, at any rate, until I went to bed.

Even if I'd stayed awake to worry about the Surgery paper I should have been wasting my time. It was a beauty. I knew pretty well all the answers, and I went ahead at a great rate, leaving the main question until last because it was, I knew, the one I could most easily answer. It was: *Outline the operative treatment, and nursing preparation and aftercare, of a patient with calculus in the common bile duct.*

There was plenty of time. I could well afford to

take ten minutes out to close my eyes and visualise the operation . . . Sir Henry's hands and Tom's, working together . . . resecting the gall-bladder, tying off, stitching up . . . I remembered clearly a classic case, a Mr Fellows, who was Chief Male Nurse at Candley Hall. After a while I wrote it all down in detail, recalling all we'd done for Mr Fellows before he'd been discharged. I remembered, too, that he'd said: 'If ever you decide to take your mental certificate, Nurse Lake, you'll be very welcome to do it at Candley, any time. I don't need references—you'll do.' I had been very gratified by that, because Candley Hall was notoriously choosy when it came to taking on SRNs for post-graduate courses.

I checked through the paper carefully before I clipped the sheets together. There, at least, was one I hadn't made a mess of, I thought. And to make doubly sure I stayed behind afterwards with the earnest little group of autopsy-fans who went over the questions with Miss Black every day. She seemed to think we hadn't done badly, too.

On Friday we had the Nursing paper, in the morning, and the Practical in the afternoon, before the *viva*. The paper was child's play compared with the ones we'd had from the consultants. After all, we were being questioned on procedures we carried out every day, and we'd have had to be pretty dim to make a botch of that. The Practical wasn't so pleasant. Miss Fingal—the Regional Nursing Officer—turned out to be a weasely martinet of a woman with a sarcastic tongue, and that didn't make things any easier. She had one or two of the set gibbering incoherently before she had done with us. She set me to lay up trolleys for aspiration, and sternal puncture, and a theatre set for hysterectomy. She sniffed over them, passed them grudgingly, and pushed the sternal puncture one over to Con Riley, the only male student in our set. 'Well, what's it for?' she barked. 'Quickly, now!'

Poor Con gawped blankly at the trolley and said he didn't know.

'Well, it isn't for catheterisation, is it?'

'Is it for lumbar puncture?' I suppose the big needle was all he had really taken in. He looked up hopefully.

'*I'm* here to ask the questions,' Miss Fingal told him. Then she swung round on me. 'All right, Nurse! Don't stand there wasting time. Move on to the other examiners.'

It was a relief, walking round the screens, to find Miss Crump from the General, and Mr Fellows from Candley. They both smiled gently, and then asked a few questions of the what-would-you-do-if variety. Mostly about different kinds of haemorrhage, and embolism, and other ward emergencies. We'd had all those drilled into us for a long time. Then Miss Crump said: 'Good. Thank you, Nurse.' And Mr Fellows leaned forward and said: 'Did the gall-stone question ring a bell, Nurse Lake?'

I said it had rung several. 'I'm afraid I was using you all through that question, Mr Fellows. But I'd not the least idea you'd be here today.'

'Telepathy,' he said. 'As long as it helped . . . Right—that's all, Nurse, thank you. And remember what I told you.'

'I will,' I promised.

Triss was waiting for me out in the corridor, talking to Mrs Inge, who was shooing people in and out in turn. She said: 'OK? Not that I thought much of Fingal.'

'Not bad,' I said. 'Wasn't it nice to see Mr Fellows again? You remember him? We might have had somebody a lot worse.'

'We certainly might. What was all that about "remember what I told you" as I went past the table?'

'Oh, he said he'd have me at Candley any time, if I ever wanted to do Mental.'

'And do you?'

'Not particularly, no. But it was nice of him.'

'I wouldn't want to go there, frankly. It must be frightfully depressing. Still, once I've got my SR, no more courses for me, chum.'

'Why not cookery?'

'Cheek!' she said. 'I *can* cook. You ask Alan. The last time I went to stay with his people—'

'That's another thing,' I brooded. 'I've never even *met* Tom's folks. And they exist, all right. They only live in Shropshire. After all this time you'd think he'd have taken me over to see them. Wouldn't you?'

'Would you?' Triss shook her head at me. 'Chaps aren't a bit like girls, you know. They have to feel very committed indeed before they take girls home to be inspected. They don't do it lightly.'

'Exactly. That's what I mean. He *isn't* committed.'

'So?' Triss looked troubled again. 'Look, you can't push it, old dear. Not really.'

'I know,' I said. 'Don't listen to me. I just feel a bit unhooked after these darned exams. I think I'll have an early night.'

She nodded. 'Yes, you do that. Go and leap into a bath and I'll stick your bottle in for you. If you ask me, you've got one of your sniffy colds coming on. You know what you are—it's nothing but a stress syndrome with you, half the time.'

That was the trouble with Triss—she was so often right.

On the way to the bathroom I decided to ring through to Tom. Mrs Keatley said he was in theatre, but she was too busy to hang on, so she'd put me through and I could ask. And then Sister Pleydell answered. She was laughing as she picked up the receiver. I didn't have the nerve to ask for him after that. I put the phone down and went on to my bath. There was plenty of time to check with him about Maggie Root's party before the next evening, after all. I wasn't even sure that I wanted to go—though most residents' parties were enormous fun—except to keep Triss company. His invitation had hardly been pressing. In fact none of his invitations had been very pressing lately. He seemed to get hung up later and later in the theatre on Tuesdays, and it was a long time since he'd been able to take a complete half-day.

CHAPTER TWO

In fact I didn't go to the party. Triss was right: by Saturday morning I had a streaming cold, and the very last thing I wanted to do was to be sociable to the residents and the ward sisters. But I managed to persuade Triss to go without me, after all. 'It's not as though you'd be in uniform,' I pointed out. 'Who on earth cares about protocol at a party these days? Besides, you can keep an eye on Tom for me . . . Oh, will you let him know I can't go?'

'Of course. I'll send him a message by Alan,' she promised. 'He'll be doing rounds this morning, I'm bound to see him. And I'll come and see you in the morning and tell you all the scandal . . . By the way, Home Sister's bringing you a hot drink or something, and she says do you want to see the SMO? Or are you just taking it easy on your morning off?'

I told her I certainly didn't want to see Dr Ridware. 'He'd have me out of here and into the sick bay, and I wouldn't get out again for a week, the old fusspot.'

'It never used to be like that, not until Paterson's people complained to the committee that she'd had pneumonia and wasn't warded until her private doctor saw her.'

'That was her own fault,' I said. 'She knew

28

darned well what sort of temp. she was running. But she wanted to stay on, so as to get her day off on the Saturday for Sister Lander's wedding. You can't blame the SMO for *that*. She didn't report sick.'

'I don't blame him. But ever since then, things have been different, you must admit. Matron used to make us feel like criminals if we went off, but now . . . well, if you were a second-year, Home Sister'd have got Dr Ridware without asking you by now. Nothing else you want? Alan's taking me to the Zoo.'

'What on earth for?

'I've never been. Why not?'

'Give my love to the monkeys,' I said. Tom had taken me to the Zoo once, and a mother monkey had brought her tiny baby to the rails to show him. She had let Tom touch it, but when I tried she bit my finger and Tom had to rush me back to Casualty to get it stitched. It had been stiff ever since when my hands were cold. The odd thing was that it was my ring finger. 'And mind you don't get bitten,' I added.

'Lord, yes. I'd forgotten that. I'll be careful.' Triss waved and closed the door behind her.

When Home Sister came in, ten minutes later, she brought a hot lemon drink, two codeine tablets, and a stack of magazines. 'I borrowed these from the pile the Friends of the Hospitals brought in this week for the patients,' she confessed. 'Well, you *are* a patient, temporarily . . . I'd better just take your temperature, dear, in case Matron asks.'

'I have,' I said. 'It was just over a hundred, that's all.'

'I see. Then keep warm, dear. And I'll look in later to see whether you feel like any lunch. You may be ready for some soup if nothing else.' She went over and fiddled with the stuff on the dressing table, tidying it, and twitched the curtains farther over the window, and then she said: 'And how did the exams go, Nurse? Not too bad?'

'Not too good, either,' I said. 'The Medicine was pretty stiff. I made a terrible bloomer—mixed up Addison's and Simmonds' diseases. I don't know what got into me.'

'Well, I should think you were cooking up this cold! I'll mention it to Miss Black, if you like. They do try to make allowances if anyone's off colour. Don't worry—I'm sure you'll be through all right . . . Goodness me, if you fail, dear, so will a lot of others.'

She bustled off in the end, and after a while I went to sleep, because when I tried to look at the magazines my eyes kept sliding about as though I had nystagmus. I slept most of the day, on and off, waking now and again when Miss Appleby came in with soup, and tea, and a fresh hot bottle.

By the evening I felt a good deal better. All the same, it seemed far too much like hard work to get dressed, so I had a hot bath and went back to bed again, and slept right through until after midnight. I woke then, hearing voices under my window, and footsteps on the gravel. There seemed to be several people coming in very late. It occurred to me that they were probably coming over from the residents' party, and I went to the window to look. There were vague shapes in a moving group on the fore-court, and Maggie Root, over-excited, was saying: 'I want to go and say goodbye to her . . . Come on, McDonough! You know the way.'

'She'll be asleep,' Triss said.

'Well, I shan't wake her!'

'No, Maggie. Go to bed. Alan—take her back with you. And for heaven's sake be quiet—you'll have us all shot at dawn.'

There was more talk that I couldn't properly hear, and then two people separated from the group and wavered away towards the residents' quarters, and the front door of the Home clicked shut. After a while I heard Triss come along the corridor and pause outside my door. 'Triss?' I said. 'I'm awake.'

She rustled in, in the dark, and sat on the edge of the bed. 'You should be asleep, my girl.'

'I have been. What was all that with Maggie, outside?'

'Oh, she wanted to come up and see you, the idiot. I told her residents weren't allowed in the harem, but she said that rule was made in the days when all residents were men. She was a bit over the edge, actually. Everyone had been pouring sherry into her, and champagne; and she isn't used to it.'

'Poor old Maggie,' I said. 'I suppose she doesn't really want to leave. She's a good sort. If I'm going to Three, let's hope her replacement's as good.'

'Johnny Heathcote? He's got it. Well, the Cas girls seem to like him. He brought Staff Coates to the party. Oh, and who *do* you think the SSO was with?'

I yawned. 'I can't imagine. Theatre Sister?'

'Oh, no. She was—No, he brought Miss Black.'

'So there *is* something in all the rumours? Well, well! Jolly good luck to her. I thought Owen Humphries was a confirmed bachelor.'

'Didn't we all? Even Staff Beddoes gave up trying long ago. And heaven knows she has plenty of opportunity, in theatre.'

'Ah, but she's got competition now,' I reminded her. 'This Pleydell is quite a dish. It's funny, all the Guy's people we get here seem to be real smashers. Is it because Guy's makes them competitive, or is it that only the dishy ones ever apply to go there, or do they only take on the best specimens?'

'Stop talking,' Triss said sharply. 'And go to sleep. I'm off.' She stood up again and smoothed the bedspread.

I held her wrist. 'Wait. You haven't told me what Tom was up to. Was he there?'

'Yes, he was there.'

Triss is a poor actress, even in the dark. Her tone of voice said it for her. 'I see. He was with Sister Pleydell. Is that it?'

'I didn't say so.'

'Oh, Triss! Somebody else will tell me, if you don't.'

'All right.' Her voice was flat. 'Yes, he was with Pleydell. You don't have to read anything into that, do you? I expect he took her out of sheer courtesy. Let's face it, all the other men are tied up.'

'And he isn't, of course?'

'Well—tonight he was at a loose end, wasn't he? It doesn't mean a thing, taking a girl to a residents' do. Not a thing.'

'Doesn't it? You made it sound mighty significant when the SSO took Miss Black.'

'That's different, Abby. You know it is. They're older, for one thing. That was—Well, after all this time it was tantamount to a public declaration. Everyone knows about you and Tom by now.'

'Everybody? You think Pleydell knows?'

'She couldn't help knowing. These things get around. There's just as much gossip in the sisters' sitting-room as there is in ours, you know.'

'Go away,' I said. 'Go to bed, Triss. Don't stand there trying to pour oil. I told you, he isn't by any means committed. Pleydell can have him, for all I care. I dare say she'd make a far better consultant's wife than ever I should. They need someone decorative to entertain for them, don't they? Maybe she has money, too, for all I know.'

Triss's voice was surprisingly tart. 'She should have. Her father's the boss man of Pleydell Plastics, isn't he? So they say. And I don't imagine that fur coat of hers came out of sister's pay, or the Spitfire she drives, even if it is second-hand. Go on, torture yourself, if that's the way you want it! I never thought you could be so dim. Working yourself into a tizzy, just because Tom was decent enough to invite a new sister to a casual get-together in the mess. It doesn't mean a thing.'

'The same applies to the SSO, then. You can't have it both ways,' I told her obstinately.

'Have it your own way.' She opened the door. 'But you've got it all wrong.'

'Time will tell,' I said. 'Goodnight, Triss.'

I lay awake for quite a long time after she had gone.

My cold had completely cleared up next morning, but Miss Appleby insisted on sending me breakfast in bed, and said: 'All right, Nurse. Go on duty if you feel fit—but as you're not due on until two o'clock you may as well lie in for a while. And don't go on unless you really feel up to it.' She frowned. 'Where is it you're going? I've forgotten.'

'Three,' I said.

'Yes. It's their take-in day, so you'll be tired before you've done. You rest while you can.'

'I feel fine,' I assured her. 'Honestly, I've been vegetating long enough in study-block. I'm itching to get back to work again.' What I meant was, I think, that I was itching to be back where I could see Tom, and know for myself what was going on. 'I've been shut up in that school for more than a month.'

'Yes, I dare say you feel out of touch . . . You know, Nurse, I'm not sure that we didn't get on better in the days before study-block was invented. We had two or three lectures a week, alongside our ward work, and we did learn as we went along. It gave us a chance to ask Tutor about things we saw during the week. Theory without practice isn't such a good thing, in my opinion. You don't relate your studies to your work in quite the same way. Still, it's not for me to question the decisions of the GNC. I suppose they know what they're doing. Thank goodness. I've only two years to go.'

I was surprised. She didn't look a day over forty-five to me, and I said as much. 'You look fifteen years too young, Miss Appleby.'

'Do I?' She laughed. 'Perhaps that's because I'm a fairly contented person, dear. I've always enjoyed my work. I'd rather be working in the wards than here, I'm afraid, but acute rheumatism put paid to that for me. I have to make the best of it. I have patients now and again, when you girls fall sick, and I enjoy looking after you. We have to do what we can in this life, and not hanker after the things we can't have. My father always used to say that the art of happy living was the art of accepting the inevitable gracefully, Nurse.'

'I dare say he was right,' I said slowly. 'Only it isn't exactly easy, is it?'

'Nothing worth while ever is, my dear . . . Well, I can't stay here chattering. I'm supposed to be taking Matron's office this morning. Remember, if you don't feel fit at lunch-time, don't go on duty. Understood?' She patted my feet under the bed-spread.

I went up to Three just before two o'clock. Sister Knight was waiting for me. 'Staff Nurse Hasan won't be back until four,' she told me. 'She's only just gone to lunch, and to get a couple of hours off, because her relief didn't turn up and we've been busy with admissions. You know it's our take-in? There's only one bed left now. Well, there are two, but one's booked for a written-for. So you can take one, and one only. All right?'

I nodded. 'Yes, Sister.'

'Mr Fitzgibbon's off until ten tonight, so Mr Heathcote's on duty. If there's anything he can't handle he'll just have to get the SSO, or bring Mr Dell in.' She slid on her cuffs and picked up her cape. 'You can read the report for yourself—it's quite straightforward. I have to go now, because I've a train to catch, and I'm late as it is. Any questions?'

'No, I'll cope, Sister,' I said. 'You carry on.'

'Keep an eye on the crash boy,' she said. 'Caldecott.' She shot off along the flat, leaving me with thirty-odd men, one second-year, and an orderly. Minnie Rogers, the Ward 3 orderly, was pretty dim, but the second-year was a girl named Williams—B. J. Williams, to distinguish her from the seven other Williamses in the Royal—who'd worked with me before, and who could move fast if she had to. I was glad about that.

At least the ward was tidy, ready for the afternoon crop of visitors, except for screens round a couple of admissions. B.J. was cutting bread and butter for the teas, out in the kitchen, and Minnie Rogers was filling a trolleyful of flower vases ready for the fresh supplies. I sat down to read the back reports, and then did a round of the ward to check on the four-hourlies and to see that the new people were comfortable.

One of the admissions looked very rough. He was a boy of eighteen, named Robin Caldecott, rushed in with multiple injuries after a motorcycle crash. They'd got him fixed up with a drip, near the door where I could watch him, and John Heathcote had written him up morphia *s.o.s.* He'd had a shot at one o'clock, and he looked as if he was already coming out of it. His blood-pressure didn't seem to be rising, and one way and another I didn't like the look of him.

I went into the kitchen to B.J. 'This boy Caldecott,' I said. 'How long is it since Mr Heathcote saw him?'

She looked up from the bread and butter. 'Getting on for an hour, I think. He seemed to be a bit windy about him, I thought.'

'So am I,' I said. 'He's a filthy colour. Dirty beige. What are they going to do about him? Sister didn't say.'

'Well, Mr Heathcote said they'd have him in theatre as soon as they'd pumped enough blood into him, Nurse. The SSO's seen him too, by the way, so—'

'If he doesn't improve, the SSO ought to see him again, and soon,' I said. 'I don't think it can wait until Staff Hasan gets back, frankly.' I still felt uneasy, and B.J. was a sensible girl. 'Look,' I said. 'You run and have a look at him. Tell me if he looks worse or better than when the HS saw him. I've only just arrived. I can't tell.'

She wiped her hands and went at once. When she came back she said: 'Worse. Well, his colour's worse. The blood doesn't seem to be helping.'

'Then that settles it,' I said. 'I thought myself he looked as if there was some internal haemorrhage going on, and I still think so. I'll ring for the HS again.'

John Heathcote was a broken reed. He frowned down at young Caldecott's notes and said: 'Don't you think he'll do?'

'What I think doesn't matter,' I said. 'You're the doctor. Personally I don't feel he will, unless something's done pronto. Why not get the SSO to take another look? His b.p.'s dropping steadily—I've just checked it again. He's haemorrhaging somewhere for sure.' I sighed. 'Do buck up. *I* can't get the SSO unless you say so.'

He touched the boy's yellow-pale face. 'Yes. He's clammy, too.' I had the impression that 'clammy' was just a word he'd read in a textbook—the way policemen always talk about speech being 'slurred', when half of them don't know what it means, or at least don't know enough to distinguish between drunken speech and that of a man who's had a cerebral thrombosis. 'I wonder,' he went on, 'do you think I ought to get Mr Dell in? The SSO's tied up just now. You see, Fitz is off till tonight, and—'

'Yes,' I said firmly. After all, somebody had to make a decision. 'Yes, get Mr Dell. They can't shoot you.'

'You'd be surprised. He won't like it. Not on a Sunday. I mean—'

'For Pete's sake!' I exploded. 'He's a surgeon. What's he *for*?'

By the time he had gone off to telephone I was already prejudiced against Mr Dell. Who did he think he was, to expect his Sundays to be free from interruption? People who wanted a nine-to-five job shouldn't become doctors. Until we had a regular consultant instead of Sir Henry Newdegate it was his job to be on call, and to come when he was sent for, exactly as Sir Henry would have done. I fumed to myself.

I checked the temporary dressings they'd put on the boy in Casualty. There wasn't much to see externally, except the leg they'd roughly set—and those dressings weren't through—and the bruising on his chest and abdomen. But his pulse was feeble, and his skin was, as John had said, downright clammy, to say nothing of that ominous pallor. I stepped up the drip as far as I could, and tipped the bed another inch or two on its gimbals. There was so little I *could* do.

'He's coming in right away,' John said through the gap in the screens. 'He didn't *seem* to mind.'

'He'd better not!' I said. 'Look, I can't speed this thing up any more. Is there anything else I can do at all? Do you want to give him a shot of anything? Levophed?'

'Yes. I'll get it. You carry on—I expect you're busy, aren't you?'

There was a little group of visitors in the corridor

waiting to be allowed in, and the telephone began to ring. 'Looks like it,' I said. 'I'll be back.'

B.J. got to the phone first. She handed it to me. 'It's Cas,' she said. 'Can we take an acute appendix?'

I took it from her. 'Nurse Lake here,' I said. 'You want us to take an appendix?'

'That's right. For op stat.' It was Harry Dane, the Casualty third-year. 'You've got beds, I gather.'

'That's all right. But no more. We're full now.'

Harry laughed shortly. 'Mate, if they come, they come. You've got at least one more bed, haven't you?'

'One,' I agreed. 'For a written-for.'

'Written-for!' Harry made a rude noise. 'OK. I'll send this fellow up, then.'

I sent B.J. to get a bed ready for him while I sorted out the visitors, and then I assembled a set of case-papers at the desk. When B.J. came back I said: 'You'll have to cope with the visitors and whatnot—tell 'em to wait for Hasan if they've got problems—if I get tied up, because Mr Dell's coming in, to look at Caldecott.'

'Oh, swell.' She smiled. 'Sunday, too. We're lucky to get him.'

'Lucky?' I said. '*Lucky!* Look, it's his job. Sunday, Monday, any day of the week. People don't get ill to the clock, or the date. If he's out playing golf, or something, that's just too bad. He's very fortunate. He might be lying dying, like Caldecott, waiting for some doctor to come in time.' B.J. was looking at me oddly, but I didn't get the message.

'Just who do these surgeons think they are? Why mustn't *they* be disturbed? Why should inexperienced youngsters like John Heathcote have to take all the responsibility?'

'Why, indeed?' someone said behind me.

He wasn't as tall as Tom, or as broad, but there was strength in every line. Compact, that was the word. And he had rough dark hair that looked as though he had just been running his fingers through it. He probably had—I was to learn later that he did that a good deal. His brown eyes looked as though they missed nothing, yet as though they could laugh at the drop of a hat. 'I don't play golf, actually,' he said. 'My name's Dell. You need me?' It was a quiet voice, but the kind that commands attention, and it had a hint of a Gloucester drawl.

B.J. shot off and left me to it, and when I had pulled myself together I said: 'Yes, sir, we do. This way . . .' and took him over to Caldecott's bed, where John Heathcote was.

He took in the situation rapidly, looked the boy over without disturbing him too much, read the Casualty notes and nodded briefly. 'Theatre,' he said. 'Right away.' He looked at me. 'Fix it, Nurse.'

John said: 'Do you think he'll stand it, sir?'

'No. But it's the only chance he has. There's no choice. Fix an anaesthetist, will you? Twenty minutes.'

That was moving, John darted off to the corridor phone, and I used the one in Sister's office. Meanwhile the appendix man was brought up, and B.J. put him to bed. Minnie got on with the tea-trolley.

and complained that it was 'all go'. By the time we'd fixed everything Mr Dell had gone. John said: 'Man of action!' and fanned himself. 'Hardly the Newdegate technique.'

'Oh, I don't know,' I said. 'He could move when he had to. Out of my way, John. I'll have to prep the boy to some extent.' I had the tray on my arm.

'Right. Theatre O.K.?'

I nodded. 'They're setting now. Anaesthetist laid on, is he?'

'Dr Chant's coming in right away.'

'And you'll assist, will you?'

'Oh, lord! I suppose I'll have to, won't I?'

'You will,' I said. 'Unless the SSO's free now. Cheer up—he looks harmless enough. Human.'

'Human dynamo, you mean,' John grumbled. 'Oh, well. As you say, they can't shoot me.'

'And what about the appendix, that's just come up? It's supposed to be for op too.'

He didn't know, he said, but he'd arrange it and let me know. Then he went upstairs.

Alfred, the theatre porter, took Caldecott up exactly twenty minutes later, while I was prepping the appendix man. He said that Mr Dell would do that afterwards, but that they'd let me know when to give the pre-med. 'Anyway, Nurse, he'll *do* it.'

'Big of him,' I said. 'But don't quote me.'

It was nearly an hour before the boy came down again. He still looked deathly, but I wasn't worried about him the way I'd been before. Alfred, who is a wise old bird like most theatre porters, said: 'He'll do, Nurse. You'll see.' And I believed him, as I always believe hospital porters. They know. Because the way sick people look is all they really know about them, they become experts in spot-diagnosis, and I would rather take an experienced porter's word as to a patient's chances than that of a junior houseman, any day. Ward sisters, too, have hunches that can be relied on.

'If you say so, Alfred,' I said. 'I'm glad to hear it.'

Staff Hasan arrived a few minutes after the appendix man had had his pre-med and gone up. 'Poor you!' she said. 'Everything happens when you get here. Never mind—make a cup of tea now, and I'll take over. I'm glad they've had Caldecott up—he looked dreadful when I went off. How is he now?'

'He'll do,' I said. 'Alfred says so.'

She had a tinkling little laugh, 'Then so it will be.'

We had cleared away the teas, and the visitors, and the fresh flowers and fruit, by the time the appendix came down again. Mr Dell, still gowned up, was helping Alfred with the trolley. He and Staff Hasan went together to Caldecott's bed. 'Well, Staff?' he asked her.

'I think he will do, sir.'

'So do I. Good. Had to take his spleen. Heathcote can write him up a sedative. Get me if you need me, hm?' He nodded to her and made for the door. I stood aside to let him pass, but he halted and looked at me as though I had a particularly interesting rash on my face. 'Name?' he wanted to know.

'Mine, sir? Lake.'

'Nurse Lake. I see. Thank you.' He walked on past me to the lift, and thumbed the button with his back to me.

It was an odd little conversation. Certainly it was the first time a consultant—or semi-consultant—had asked my name. I told Staff Hasan about it when she came for her cup of tea in the kitchen. 'Now why did he ask me that?' I wondered.

She smiled her secret little smile. 'Because he wants to know, I suppose. Perhaps he wants to report you for something you did wrong?' She was teasing. 'Or perhaps you were very rude to him?'

'But I didn't—'

'No, of course not. What do I know of his mind? I have seen him only twice. Still, we shall see much more of him.'

'For a bit, I suppose.'

'For a long time.'

'Oh?'

She nodded. 'Sister Knight is telling me that he has the appointment. In the bag, as she says.'

I was horrified. 'Are you *sure*, Staff?'

'Oh, yes. It was fixed at last night's meeting. Mr Fitzgibbon has told her, I think.'

Mr Fitzgibbon had not seen fit to tell *me*, I reflected. Then I wanted to kick myself. 'Poor Tom,' I said. 'I think he'd set his heart on it. What on earth can I say to him?'

Hasan was troubled. 'Oh, he is your friend! I am so sorry. I had forgotten. He will be very disappointed?'

'Very, I think. He said that if he didn't get it he

should probably leave Middleton in any case. It was his one chance of an appointment in these parts.'

'I am sorry. Truly.' She put her little brown hand on my arm. 'I should perhaps have said nothing. Forgive me.'

'It's all right. I had to know some time.'

'I suppose so . . . I think Mr Dell will be a good man, though. Don't you?'

'I dare say. But you couldn't expect Tom to stay on as his registrar. Not after—'

'It would hurt his pride?'

'Obviously. And there's no other vacancy to come up here for a long time, so he'd do better to go, I suppose.'

'Perhaps so,' Hasan agreed. 'Now, will you go and stay with the little Caldecott, and let Nurse Williams go to tea?'

I rang at nine o'clock before I went in to supper, but Tom was still out. I tried again at ten from the Home, and again at ten-thirty. The last time he was in theatre, the night porter said. Could he ring me? 'Not after eleven,' I underlined. 'Or I'll be in trouble with Miss Appleby.'

He rang just after five minutes to eleven, sounding far more buoyant than I had expected him to do. 'Just knocked off,' he apologised. 'Was there something?'

'Oh, Tom,' I said. 'I'm *so* sorry!'

He didn't react. 'About what?'

'The—the consultancy. I heard this afternoon. Why on earth didn't you tell me?'

'Didn't know until this morning, love. What chance have I had? Not to worry. There'll be others.'

'Yes, but not here. Not for ages . . . So I suppose—I suppose you'll be moving on? That's what you said.'

'Oh, no, not immediately. I could learn a lot from Dell, from what I've seen of his work so far. Abby, I told you, on Tuesday. He's a fantastic surgeon.'

I was astounded. 'You mean to say you'll stay on here and work *under* him? After he's pipped you to the appointment? I never thought—'

'Why not? The best man got it, in my opinion. Hell, I don't have to be small-minded about it!'

I was annoyed. 'You didn't even tell me he'd applied.'

Tom whistled. 'Lovey, I did. I told you on Tuesday that I didn't think I could stand up to the competition, but you kept telling me not to talk shop . . . Look, Dell's well qualified, and he's written a couple of darn good textbooks too. *I* don't mind working under him, not if it'll teach me anything. Why should I? Or do you want to get rid of me, is that it?'

'You know that isn't true,' I said. 'I don't want you to leave—but I just didn't think you'd stay in the circumstances. I was *frightfully* disappointed for you.'

'Oh, you take it all too seriously . . . How's that cold of yours, Abby? Better?'

I had been wondering when he would ask. 'Much

better, thanks. I went on duty today.'

'Where are you?'

'If you'd been on yourself, you'd know! Three. With nobody but John Heathcote to lean on. We could have done with you. He had to get Mr Dell in.'

'Ah, then you've met him? What did you think?'

What did I think? It was hard to say. 'I'm not sure. He makes an impact, I'll say that much. He's abrupt, too. But I suppose he's—well, an exciting sort of person.'

'There you are, you see! Even you could feel it. He's a hell of a chap.'

Hero-worship wasn't in Tom's line at all, and it bewildered me. I said: 'Well, maybe I'll see you on the ward, tomorrow?'

'I expect so. Oh, incidentally—I've changed my half-day. Tuesday isn't all that clever, not with Dell's list in the morning. Half the time I don't get off until well after lunch. So I've swopped with Alan, and I'm having Thursdays from now on. It'll be a lot better.'

Thursday was Staff Hasan's day off, always. It would be quite impossible for me to take it as a half-day, because I would have to deputise for her, as the senior third-year. '*Must* it be Thursday, Tom?'

'Afraid it's fixed now, yes. Why?'

'I'll never be able to have it. It's Hasan's day off. She's always had it, and she won't want to swop. And with Sister Knight going off at five—well, it means I have to be there.'

'Oh, rough luck.' Tom sounded almost impatient. 'Never mind. We'll work something out. All right?'

'All right,' I said bleakly. 'Goodnight, Tom.'

I looked in on Molly when I saw that her light was still on. She was sitting up in bed, in a neatly buttoned blue bedjacket, swotting up *Modern Theatre Techniques*. 'How goes the ivory tower?' I asked her. 'Taken any cases yet?'

'Oh, yes.' She was flushed with pleasure. 'I took an appendix today, for Mr Dell. Wasn't it from Three? An emergency?'

'That's right.'

'Sister said I had done very well.'

'Was she on, then? On Sunday?'

'Oh, yes. She has Thursday off for her whole day, and then half days on—'

'*She* has Thursday?'

'Why, yes.'

'I see. Since when? Sister Bradshaw always had Sunday and Monday, when she was there.'

'Since last week, I think. She's only just got herself organised, I suppose. Well, she's only been here three weeks.'

It seemed to me that in only three weeks Sister Pleydell had managed to cover quite a lot of ground. 'She's arranged things nicely, hasn't she?'

Molly didn't understand, but she reacted to my tone of voice. 'Don't you *like* her, Abby?'

'Not much,' I said truthfully. 'Do you?'

'She seems very sweet. Very quiet, really.'

Hero-worship seemed to be fashionable. 'You're

as bad as Tom,' I said. 'He's developed a crush on Mr Dell, for some reason, and now you're plugging Sister Pleydell . . . It's a great pity those two paragons don't get together. They sound perfect for one another!'

'But, Abby—'

'Oh, don't let's pursue it.'

Molly had a little frown line digging into the top of her button of a nose. 'Are you sure you feel better?' she said at last. 'You don't *look* too good.'

I felt a heel then for snapping at her. 'Oh, I'm still a bit under the weather. Sorry to be crotchety. I felt better for going on duty, actually. I hate kicking my heels. Goodnight, Molly. I'll get to bed.'

'Goodnight,' she said. Then: 'Abby, if you'd like some vitamin B, I've got a bottle of Cytacon you can have. It does buck you up.'

She was a nice girl. It was simply that she didn't understand.

CHAPTER THREE

EITHER the management committee or its printer
had moved fast, because we had the new case-
papers for Mr Dell's patients by Tuesday morning.
All our consultants had different colours, to make
them easily identifiable in a mixed ward. Sir
Henry's had been lilac, and we'd assumed that
Mr Dell's would be the same, but they turned out
to be buttercup yellow. They had MR SIMON
DELL across the top in bold capitals, whereas the
old ones had read: *Sir Henry Newdegate* in thin
italic script.

'Saucy,' Sister Knight said with one eyebrow
lifted. 'Oh, very saucy. Still, lilac is hardly Mr Dell,
is it? He's a pretty emphatic person. Direct. Scarcely Sir Henry's old-world bedside manner, either
. . . Here you are, Nurse Lake. Put them in the
drawer, will you, and when you have time you can
see that this week's admissions have them substituted. As from Sunday, that is. Better wait until
after the round, now.'

I glanced up at the clock. 'And what time will
that be, Sister? Tennish?'

'Half past nine, prompt, if I know him! What is
it? Nine now. You'd better slip off for coffee,
Nurse, and then get back to see to things here.
Staff'll be busy with dressings, so you'd better

50

follow the band.' She lifted that critical eyebrow again—she only used both when she was surprised, and that was not often—and added: 'And change your cap, Nurse. That one looks as if a horse had sat on it.'

I raced over to the Home, made my bed, changed my cap and folded up a clean apron, and hurried back to the canteen for coffee. Several of the housemen were there, but not Tom or Alan. John Heathcote was just leaving to lie in wait for Mr Dell in the front hall. I supposed that Tom would be on his way there too. It was nearly time for me to move, but I made myself sit down and finish my coffee first. If I hadn't, I shouldn't have run into Simon Dell along the bottom corridor as I went back.

He nodded briefly. ''Morning, Nurse Lake.'

I said: 'Good morning, sir.'

'Seen that houseman of mine?'

'I think he'll be in the hall, sir. He was on his way there a minute ago.'

He grunted. 'Miss Root never waited in the hall. She met me in the car park.'

I looked out through the window beside us. The rain was coming down in great windblown swirls. 'With an umbrella, sir?'

It wasn't meant to sound pert, but it obviously did, because his dark eyebrows practically met for a second. Then he began to laugh. And because he had an unexpectedly infectious chuckle, so did I. When Tom came chasing through from the hall with his white coat flying behind him we were both standing there wet-eyed, like a couple of tittering juniors.

Tom pulled up with a sideways slide, as if he were on skates. 'Something funny, sir?'

'Yes, Tom. This girl here. Nurse Lake.'

'I see, sir.' Tom looked at me hard. 'I see.'

'Yes.' Simon Dell gave me the ghost of a wink, the merest flicker of his left eye, and straightened his face. 'Well? Ready for rounds? I've been here at least five minutes.'

I let them get ahead of me, walking towards the lift, and then I skipped up the stairs and raced them to Ward 3. By the time the two of them reached the ward door I had alerted Sister Knight, sent Minnie Rogers out into the sluice-room with her mop and bucket, and swept the disobedient litter of magazines from the appendix man's bed. John Heathcote came panting in as they reached the second patient. Mr Dell looked up from Caldecott's notes. 'You're late, Heathcote. My round begins at nine-thirty, not nine-forty-five.'

'Sorry, sir.' John pushed back his red flop of hair. 'Must have missed you somewhere downstairs.'

'You must.' He moved to the next bed, a written-for hernia dressed ready for theatre, and picked up the notes. 'Sister, who made out these case-papers?'

She moved her eyes but not her head. 'You, Nurse?'

'Yes, Sister. Is there anything wrong, sir?'

'No . . . no.' He didn't sound too sure. 'Odd sort of handwriting, that's all . . . Now, Mr Harker, we'll be having you up to the theatre in about twenty minutes' time. Just relax. Nurse will give you an injection in a moment.' He turned to me. 'Let him have his pre-med.'

Sister nodded, and I fetched the hypo tray, filled the syringe and held it up with the ampoule for Sister to check, shot the atropine and scopolamine into Mr Harker's arm, swabbed it off, and crossed the dose out on his notes. Mr Dell watched every move. Then he said: 'Ever *had* an injection, Nurse?'

I nodded. 'Yes, sir. Well, I've been practised on with sterile water by the juniors.'

'Did it hurt?'

'Sometimes, sir.'

'Then justice was done. *Stab* your needle in, Nurse. You're not bodging holes for *broderie anglaise*. Human skin's tough stuff. Leather. It doesn't prick like a balloon.'

Sister Knight was startled, Tom was frowning, and I was annoyed as well as feeling sick. I was practically a staff nurse: I didn't expect to have my techniques criticised in front of the patients. And I wondered what on earth Mr Dell knew about *broderie anglaise*. 'I'm sorry, sir,' I said stiffly. 'Sorry if it hurt, Mr Harker.'

'It didn't, love,' Mr Harker said peaceably. 'Don't you fret. If that was the worst I had to bear . . .'

Mr Dell had already moved on to the next bed. He finished the round in a quarter of an hour flat, and I stood holding a clean towel for him while he scrubbed his hands at the outgoing basin. Tom and Sister were conferring at the desk, and John Heathcote was at the far end of the ward, catching up with some notes. When Mr Dell straightened up and held out his hands for the towel he said, very gently: 'Sulking?'

I shook my head. 'No, sir.'

'Look, I said what I did to make you *remember*. You will.'

'Yes, I will, sir,' I told him. 'But I don't seem to be doing anything right today, do I? My hypos are all wrong—and that, I may say, was because the needle was blunt and the new issue hasn't come up—and my handwriting's "odd", and—'

He finished drying his hands and pushed the towel into mine. 'All right, don't scowl. It spoils your nice face.' Then he walked smartly up the ward and took Tom away with him to the theatre.

'Well!' Sister Knight said. 'Quite the little whirlwind this morning, aren't we? It used to take Sir Henry close on an hour to do the round. Will you ask Minnie to make my coffee now, Nurse? Then you can take up the hernia.'

'Me, Sister?'

'Who else? Nurse Williams is off; Staff's busy; Nurse Phillips has all her locker-tops to do yet. I can't send Minnie or Mrs Johnston, can I?'

'What about the four-hourlies, Sister?'

'I'll do those myself. It gives me a chance to talk to the patients. Run along, Nurse . . . He won't eat you!'

When Alfred came down with his trolley I helped

Mr Harker on to it—he was fairly drowsy by then—and collected his notes, and a receiver with tongue forceps, peg and airway, and shoved it under his pillow, and followed him into the lift. Dr Chant, the anaesthetist, was waiting in the anteroom, and when Mr Harker had blacked out under pentothal he helped me to wheel the trolley through into theatre.

I was butting my way backwards through the doors with the empty trolley when Sister Pleydell widened her china-blue eyes above her mask. I pushed the last foot of trolley through and went back to stand behind her. 'Yes, Sister?'

She turned her turbanned head slightly, watching Tom clip the towels. 'Stay, Nurse. Mr Dell likes two dirty nurses, and I've only Mr Riley until Nurse Leonard comes back.'

It wasn't usual, but I nodded and stood back against the wall. Con Riley winked at me from the opposite side and inclined his head towards Mr Dell. His eyes said: 'Watch this.'

It was an education. I don't know how long they took over that hernia, but it must have been less than ten minutes. And all through the tiniest incision I had ever seen—not much more than an inch. His hands were as quick and neat as a woman's. When he had inserted a clip, and stood back, Tom said: 'Nice work, sir. Record time, too, I should think.'

'Speed's important, Tom. Yes, I know I've said it before. I'm always preaching about it. Less time taken, less shock to the patient. That's why elderly surgeons become killers. Not because they're clumsy, or because they do damage: because they're *slow*. Ought to retire at forty-five from active operating. I shall. Nurse Lake, you can take the patient now.'

When I ran the trolley along the ward for the next patient Sister came to help me and said: 'Where on earth have you been, Nurse?'

'Sister Pleydell asked me to stay. Apparently Mr Dell insists on a spare nurse up there.'

'Does he, indeed? Then he'd better do a little recruiting! I can't have my ward held up like this.'

'It *was* only ten minutes or so, Sister.'

'Well, this time you come straight back. Clear?'

'Yes, Sister. And if—'

'If there's any trouble I'll see Mr Dell myself.'

There was trouble. This time he stopped my getaway with: 'Where are you going, Nurse Lake?'

'Back to the ward, sir,' I said. 'Sister needs me.'

'So do I. Especially during this case.'

'I'm sorry, sir, but—'

He stood there with his gloved hands held at shoulder level and looked at me steadily. He had longer lashes than Triss. 'Nurse—'

'Sir?'

'Tell me something. Whose ward are you from—mine, or Sister Knight's?'

'Well, yours, sir.'

'And who is ultimately responsible for the patients in it, Nurse?'

'I suppose you are, sir.'

'Quite. Now stand behind Sister and keep your eyes open!'

It was no use. I went back to the tiled wall. I had long ago cultivated the art of leaning on walls while appearing to stand vertically. It's an art—a necessary one—perfected by every nurse who has to spend long hours in theatre.

When he got down to the liver and exposed the gall bladder he looked up. 'Now, Nurse Lake . . . Yes, and you, Riley. I want you to watch this.' We stepped nearer, and watched him slit the common bile duct and milk out the stone, and then insert a T-tube. Then he began to stitch up. When he got to the skin sutures he said: 'Well? What did I do?'

Con said: 'Removed a calculus from the common bile duct, sir.'

'Anything else?' He was looking at me.

'Put in a T-drain, sir.'

'That all? Sure?'

'Yes, sir, I think so.'

'You didn't by any chance see me resect the gall-bladder? Or did you?'

We both shook our heads.

'I just wondered. And what is the name of this operation?'

Con and I frowned at one another and said nothing.

'Choledochotomy. Remember that, will you? All right, Nurse Lake. You can go. Riley can see the patient down.'

'What now?' Sister Knight wanted to know, in the ward. 'Did he keep you? Or have you been gossiping with the anaesthetist all this time? Just wait till I see Master Dell . . . That next man needs socks before he goes up, Nurse.'

When Con came down with Mr Litherland, the gall-stone man, I said: 'What was all that in aid of, do you imagine?'

'Not a clue . . . Unless—Oh, *lord*! Do you suppose he's marking the surgery papers instead of Sir Henry?'

I thought about it as we got Mr Packer on to the trolley. Then I said: 'That *could* be it. But if *he's* marking the papers . . . Well, I gave cholecystectomy for that question. Did you?'

'Of course I did. That's what Sir Henry always did. I've never even *seen* a chole—What was it? Choledochotomy. I've never seen one done before, have you?'

'Never,' I said. 'Not by Sir Henry, or Mr Lewis, or any of our surgeons. It's not fair if he's marking Sir Henry's papers, is it? I mean, their ideas are entirely different.' In the lift, going up, I said: 'Look, Con—How would he know they were our papers? I mean, we don't put our names on, only our numbers. That's to drill us for the State, I suppose.'

'That's a point,' Con conceded. 'Unless it was that we all gave the same answer. I dare say we did.'

'But even then, he wouldn't know which set you and I belonged to. How could he? I doubt whether he knows a third-year from a second yet. You'd be surprised how long it takes fresh people to learn all the belt-colours and so forth. And even then there'd be three sets to choose from. He *couldn't* know.'

'Unless he recognised the handwriting. He might know mine—I've written scrips for him to sign in theatre now and again, request forms for biopsies and so on. He doesn't always leave them for Fitz.'

I remembered uncomfortably what Mr Dell had said about my handwriting during the ward round. 'That's it,' I said. 'He told me mine was "odd" when he saw it on a case-paper. *That's* how he knew. But he must have a phenomenal memory, if he can keep things like that in his head.'

'He's phenomenal, all right,' Con agreed. 'Oh, yes, he's phenomenal. Old Fitz is no end impressed, you can see that. He's properly sitting at the feet of the *maestro*.'

'And well he may,' I said. 'If the *maestro* can always operate the way he's doing today.' I lugged open the lift gates and took my end of the trolley. 'Anyhow, we all know who'll land the surgery prize, so there's no point in the rest of us flogging ourselves to death.'

'Molly Leonard?'

'I should think so. She's swotted harder than any of us. She's a natural when it comes to exams. If I scrape through with sixty per cent I'll be satisfied. That's worth seventy-five in the State, so the story runs.'

This time Molly was there, and as soon as Mr Packer was out far enough to let go of my hands Dr Chant said: 'OK. You can slide off now if you want to. I can cope and Alfred will bring him back.' The

odd thing was that I was genuinely disappointed. I
wanted to go on watching Mr Dell at work. As Tom
said, there was plenty to be learned from him. It
was not only that: he had such vitality. It was a
warmth, a kind of animal magnetism, I suppose,
that I had never encountered before. It was more
than the glow of health and cleanliness that radi-
ated from Tom, and it seemed to be something he
could intensify at will. A kind of power, I tried to
explain to Triss at lunch. 'I suppose you'd call him
"dynamic",' I said. 'Even when you hate him you
can still get the impact.'

She said I made him sound like Dracula, or
Rasputin, or somebody, but that wasn't at all what I
meant.

It was the first Tuesday half-day that I'd had to
spend alone for a long time. Even when Tom had
been late finishing in theatre we had always gone
out in the evening, and it was odd to go off at two
with no idea how I meant to spend the rest of the
day.

I soaked in a hot bath while I thought about it. I
couldn't get home to Northumberland except on
nights-off and during holidays; all my local friends
were in hospital. Triss would be out with Alan if she
was able to get off—though with Sister Haywood,
in 8, that might not be easy. Sister Haywood was an
ex-QA and as tough as they came, and as far as she
was concerned you got your off-duty when you got
it, and if it didn't suit you that was too bad. Still, if
anyone could charm her, Triss could. Her ability to

talk people round was perhaps the only trace she showed of her Irish ancestry. At all events, if Triss was free she would not be going anywhere with me, that was definite. Molly was still on duty in theatre, and there was nobody else I much wanted to see. Most hospital groups are pretty clannish, and we were stuck with one another, after three years. It was difficult to form casual relationships with other people, who had their own long-standing groups.

Then the brainwave hit me. For a long time I had been promising myself a proper course of driving lessons. Tom had said it was far better to learn from a professional, and that if he went on teaching me I should pick up all his worst faults, but I had never been sure enough of regular off-duty to make appointments for lessons. If I was now to have a regular half-day, on which Tom was tied up, I was in a position to begin. I certainly didn't want to fritter the time away to no purpose.

'Call me Jeff,' the instructor said. He was a pale young man with a grubby collar. 'Everybody does . . . Now look, if you've had a few odd lessons already, there's no point in giving you the kindergarten stuff, is there? Have you driven in traffic?'

I said I had, a few times. 'But it's reversing into spaces, and doing three-point turns, and all that, that foxes me. Manoeuvring, I suppose you'd call it. I can drive straight along roads all right, but I'm hopeless at parking and so forth.'

'Right. Well, let's see you do a spot of straight

driving to begin with. Up past the hospital, round the shops, and back here again. Right?'

'Do you mean turning left after the shop block, Mr—'

'Call me Jeff,' he repeated. 'Yes, you've got the idea.' He turned to look back over my shoulder. 'Off you go, then, and don't forget your mirror.'

I managed the run round the block all right. The only trouble was that I turned too soon, and found myself back above the hospital instead of outside the driving school office. 'But that was a one-way street, surely?' I said.

'It was. You got to watch it, baby. No good me telling you when you'd done it, was it?' Call-me-Jeff looked back along the road. 'Well, it's clear. Nice little chance to do a U-turn in the road, eh?'

Getting across the road presented no difficulty. What I hadn't allowed for was the ambulance that suddenly cut in on me and then stopped dead for no apparent reason instead of turning in at the OP gate. The reson became apparent when I pulled out defensively to overtake. The ambulance hadn't been able to turn in because there was a car coming out. The long mean bonnet of a white E-type was about to cross my bows at speed.

I stood on everything—including Call-me-Jeff's foot which was already on the clutch pedal as he snatched the handbrake. So, evidently, did the E-type's driver. We came to rest about half an inch apart. 'Stupid idiot!' I jerked out. 'Fancy surging out like that! If our brakes hadn't been good— What on earth is he hooting for?'

'For you to get out of the way, I should think. Want me to take over?'

'Do,' I said. I am not at all athletic, but I scrambled over the back of my seat to let Call-me-Jeff slide across, and kept my face turned away as we moved forward. We parked outside the office again, because he said we needed a cup of tea after all that.

Only before we could get inside, the white E-type pulled in ahead of us and the driver came marching back. He stuck his head in at the window and said: 'I don't know what kind of driving school you run, but—'

'Sorry, old chap,' Call-me-Jeff said. 'The ambulance was blocking the view, see.'

Then Mr Dell saw me. 'Oh, it's you, Nurse Lake. Now if *you'd* been driving I'd have understood it.'

'I was,' I confessed.

'I see. And is your lesson over now?'

Call-me-Jeff looked at me. 'Might as well call it a day, now. Not in the mood, are you?'

Simon Dell opened the back door. 'Then I suggest you come with me, and try to learn a few of the basic facts of good driving!'

'With—with you?' I said. 'But—'

'Don't argue.' He held the door wide. 'Come along. You're wasting time.'

He wasn't a man you argued with: either you obeyed, or the floor opened and swallowed you up, it seemed to me. I got into the low seat of the E-type, and in no time at all we were out of the traffic and into a quiet maze of residential roads. 'It was the ambulance driver's fault,' I burst out at last. 'He didn't wave me down, so I simply went round him. It was that or crash into him. What else could I do?'

'You *could* have asked yourself whether it was possible that another ambulance was on its way out. You knew very well they wouldn't have stopped right outside the gate if they could have driven straight in.'

Then I lost my temper. 'Mr Dell, if you came out of that gate so fast that—so unexpectedly that the ambulance driver didn't have time to signal and simply had to slam on his brakes, then it seems to me that all this is *your* fault. Why on earth were you in such a hurry? I won't be blamed like this. I'm not a stupid driver—I do try to be careful. Anyhow, it wasn't *my* idea to do a U-turn just there.'

'I should hope not!'

'And it's not as though any damage had been done, is it? Besides—' I ran out of breath and nerve simultaneously.

'Yes?' he said patiently. 'I'm listening.'

'Well . . . I don't see why a doctor needs a high-performance sports car in a place like Middleton.'

'Now there's something I can argue about! That remark was a piece of sheer prejudice, wasn't it? Like a lot of other woolly-thinking people you've got hold of the idea that drivers buy high-performance cars simply in order to rush about at a hundred and twenty miles an hour at every possible opportunity. Yes?'

I stuck to my guns this time. 'Well, don't they? What's the point of buying a fast car unless you intend to drive it fast? It'd be a waste of money, wouldn't it?'

'Oh dear!' He laughed shortly. 'I can see I shall have to educate you . . . You know, I think we'd better go and have a meal somewhere, and then I can concentrate on what I'm saying. Have you ever been to the Willow Tree?'

'Yes, but—No, not there.'

'You don't like it?'

'I like it,' I said. 'But it's sure to be full of people from the Royal, and—'

'And you'd rather not be seen with me?'

'On the contrary, Mr Dell. It wouldn't do for *you* to be seen with *me*.' He must be dim, I thought, if he couldn't see that for himself.

He evidently was dim, because his eyebrows went up and he said: 'Why on earth not?'

'Well . . .' It must have sounded feeble. 'Well, consultants *don't* go about with third-year students. It's not on.'

He was amused. 'I see. So the poor consultants are doomed to consorting with nothing but matrons and administrators? That's rough, don't you think?' He forgot to allow for the ward sisters altogether.

I had just worked something out. 'Actually, Mr Dell, I believe you're the first bachelor consultant we've ever had. In my time, anyhow.' Because he didn't say anything I looked up at him. 'You're *not* married, are you?'

'I'm a widower, Nurse Lake . . . Oh, I can't call you "Nurse Lake" when we're off duty. It's absurd. What's your first name?'

'Annabel,' I said. 'But people call me Abby.'

'Do they? I prefer Annabel.'

'Please yourself,' I said. 'That's what my father calls me, actually.'

'And my father calls me Simon. Do you think you could manage that?'

I sighed. 'It's still easier to say "sir".'

'If you call me "sir" in the Willow Tree the waiter'll think you're my secretary, or something.'

'He won't,' I corrected him. 'He knows perfectly well that I'm Nurse Lake, who goes in there with Mr Fitzgibbon who patched up his stomach! So that's that.'

'Fitzgibbon, eh? But I thought—Is this a serious attachment?'

There was no reason why I should answer that one, but I found myself saying: 'To be frank, I'm not sure. It used to be.'

'I see.'

'But you don't,' I said. 'You don't know anything about me at all. Snap-diagnosis isn't always a good thing.'

He slowed the car and turned his head for a moment to glance at me. 'Forgive me, but I know a great deal about you. Shall I tell you some of the things I know? First, you have hazel eyes with rather long lashes—which you do not, I'm pleased to see, embellish. You have small square hands with spatulate fingertips. You have almost illegible tiny square handwriting. It looks pretty until you come to read it, but—'

'So it *was* the handwriting,' I said. 'You did recognise it! I might have known.'

'I don't think I know what you mean.'

'I mean,' I said bluntly, 'that you're marking—or you're about to mark—the surgery papers set by Sir Henry.'

He withdrew—it was like a light going out—and speeded up the car again so that it seemed to leap forward as silently as a tiger. 'I don't think we should discuss that, do you?'

'Probably not,' I said. 'But when you did that choledochotomy—'

'Shall we talk about something else?'

'Such as?' I said.

'Such as why people drive high-performance cars. Now, you've been in this one for a quarter of an hour. Have I exceeded the speed limit?'

'No, but—'

'Have you observed how very manoeuvrable the car is in traffic?'

'I grant you that,' I said grudgingly.

'Then tell me why it's better than the one that you were driving, for example.'

'I suppose it has better acceleration.'

'Quite. And more flexibility. And far better brakes. In fact, any decent sports car is a good deal *safer* to drive than a family saloon can begin to be. It's under better control. And it usually has better visibility too. *Now* do you see the point of having it for town driving?'

'I hadn't thought of it that way,' I admitted. 'I suppose you're right.'

'I *know* I'm right! Even a beginner could drive this car a lot more safely than he can drive an ordinary saloon. Want to try?'

'Heavens, no,' I said. 'I'd be scared stiff!'

'Prejudice again. You build up this image in your mind of a "fast" car—and you don't *have* to go fast in it. Believe me, it turns far more sweetly at low speeds than any of your "safe" little family cars.'

'I'll believe you,' I said. 'But I don't feel any urge to prove it to myself.'

'Look at it now—in top gear, and moving very gently. And you can't hear the engine at all, can you? . . . Well, here's the Willow Tree. Shall we risk it?'

There didn't seem to be any hospital cars outside. 'Very well,' I said. 'But if the grapevine has our names linked, don't blame me.'

'I won't, Annabel.' He sounded exactly like my father, except that my father would scarcely have looked at me in quite that way. My face was hot for a moment. That was idiotic, but I couldn't help it. He had the most searching eyes I had ever seen. It would not have surprised me if he could see clean through my head and out at the back to where his car was parked.

We were late for tea and early for dinner, but they produced steak for him and a Spanish omelette for me, and then left the Stilton with us. It was leisurely and pleasant, after all, and Simon went on talking about cars. He obviously knew a great deal about them, and he seemed to have done a good deal of competition driving at some point. We had Drambuie with our coffee and then he said abruptly: 'I have to get back to the hospital for a short time. When are you due back?'

'Oh, any time before midnight—but I meant to go back early and wash my hair and so on.'

'Your hair looks all right to me.'

'I dare say. But it's been in the wards and the theatre for two days, and it needs washing.'

'And does that take the whole evening? If you're free, we could go on somewhere else, after I've done this call.'

'I'll think about it,' I promised. 'Back in a moment.'

I hadn't spotted anyone I knew, but the restaurant was full of secluded booths, and the first person I saw in the ladies' room was a girl named Fletcher who was in my set. She saw me in the mirror as she was doing her face and turned round. 'Well, you *rat*!' she said. She meant it, too. 'No wonder you're being tipped for the Surgery prize. I didn't think you could be so crafty, Lake.'

'Don't be absurd,' I told her. 'I just happened to run into him.' She didn't know how true that had nearly been. 'And what do you mean, crafty? As for the Surgery prize, you must be potty. Leonard'll get it, hands down, any fool knows that much.'

'Yes?' She snapped the lid of her compact. 'He'll be marking the papers, won't he?'

I was furious. 'I've no idea. We haven't discussed it.'

'No. Well, you wouldn't, would you? You'd have to use a bit of subtlety. Tell him how much depends on it, and all that. At least, that's what I'd do, given the chance.' She stretched her mouth in a grin as she put on lipstick, and then pursed it and considered the effect. 'I will say, you're quick off the mark, and serve Fitz right, too. That Pleydell woman doesn't give anyone a chance. Do you know, the other night—'

'I don't know, and I don't want to know,' I said rudely. 'If I were you, Fletch, I'd make sure of my facts before I talked.'

I was still bristling when I got back to Simon, and I suppose he could see it, because he said: 'When you've recovered your equanimity, can we discuss spending the rest of the evening together? I'm a passable dancer, if that's any use.' He waved away the waiter bringing his change. 'Is it?'

I got to my feet. 'Sorry. I'd like to go straight back.'

'I see. Your feet are killing you. Well, you don't have to dance. We could—'

'We don't have to do anything,' I said. 'I ought never to have come. It was a mistake.'

He frowned thoughtfully as we made for the door, and outside he said: 'Who has said what? Did you meet someone in the cloakroom? Or on the way to it?'

'I did. And by tomorrow it'll be all round the hospital, if I know her.'

'So?'

'Can't you *see* what they think?'

'Frankly, no.' He unlocked the car and shut me in, and came round to the driver's seat with: 'What *do* they think?'

'I'll tell you,' I said. 'They think I'm trying to make sure of a good mark for the Surgery paper. *Now* do you understand?' He still looked blank. 'They think I'm currying favour.'

He sounded incredulous. 'Do they? Then they can't have much opinion of your integrity. Or mine, either. It was obviously a woman's idea, that. No man would entertain such an idea. I don't know why you bother to react to it.'

'No? You don't have to live in a female community!'

'In fact, what you're saying is that you don't want to see me again until after the results are published. That it?'

'I don't want to see you again at all. I'm sorry.'

He turned his head to look at me before he drove off. In the light from the car-park lamp his face was still and serious. 'You're quite sure about that?' he asked quietly.

'Quite sure, Mr Dell.'

'Simon,' he said.

'All right—Simon. For the last time. After this, it's "sir".'

'I shall ask you again, you know.'

'That's up to you.'

'After the results are posted, of course.'

I didn't say anything.

He drove me back quickly and efficiently, and I saw that the E-type would probably be a great asset in an emergency. That hadn't struck me before. He dropped me at the gate, as I asked him to, and I thanked him, and that was that.

I went up and washed my hair, and when it was dry I went over to the canteen. Triss and Alan were sitting there—Triss in mufti and Alan in his white coat. 'Can you beat it?' Triss said. 'We hadn't been out an hour before he was called back. Really, this *place*! You'd never think the juniors were qualified, the way they panic.'

'Well, old Hai got windy,' Alan explained. 'You know what Orientals are. I couldn't very well refuse. And where have you been?'

'Washing my hair,' I said.

'You weren't in an hour ago,' Triss told me. 'I went up to look for you while my dear fiancé was doing his houseman's work for him, and your coat wasn't there, so—'

'I went and had a driving lesson. I thought it was high time I did something about it.'

Triss grinned. 'No wonder the yard's full of ambulances! Now I understand.'

'That's right,' I said. 'I've been mowing them down, right left and centre. You know me. . . . Well, if Tom's having Thursdays off I've got to find something to occupy me, and I suppose it's good for trade.'

Alan was troubled. 'But I thought you'd change, too. I thought—Oh, look, we can swop back again. Can't we, Triss?'

'I don't know. Sister Haywood isn't the changeable type. Same off-duty list, week in, week out.

Saves her writing a fresh one, I think. If she *can* write.'

'Leave it,' I said. 'It wasn't my idea. Sister Knight can't do anything either, because Hasan always has Thursdays. Babysits for her brother, or something of the sort.'

Triss was still puzzled. 'Then why did Tom want to change?'

I still felt feline about it. 'There *are* those who have Thursdays. Like Sister Pleydell, for example!'

'You're crazy!' Triss exploded. 'She's *married*. Molly told me. I made sure she'd tell you too.'

I was genuinely startled. 'Are you sure?'

'Of course I'm sure. Pleydell told Molly, and she told me. Well, Molly's seen her husband. He's at the University. He's doing his Ph.D. thesis, and that's why she's working, to help out his grant. He's a biologist or something, doing research on insect pests. He's got a grant from some insecticide firm, as well as his scholar's dole—they'll take him on eventually, I suppose—but it isn't really enough for them to live on.'

'Oh, my best cap!' I said. 'I've been an idiot, haven't I?'

Alan nodded. 'You certainly have. I suppose you heard about his taking her to the party for Maggie, and put two and two together and made seven and a half? Muggins! She's very attractive, but she's not the two-timing kind. At least, I don't think so.'

'Then why did he want to change to Thursdays?'

He shrugged. 'Better ask him.'

That was the last thing I intended to do. He had

given me one explanation, and I'd accepted it. 'He *said* it was because of always being late getting off from theatre. Only I didn't believe him.'

'Pity,' Alan said. 'Then you'll just have to apologise, won't you? Now's your chance. He's just come down.' He was looking over my shoulder towards the door.

'I can't. He didn't *know* I didn't believe him, you ass.'

'Well? No harm in being extra nice to him, is there?'

I hesitated, and then I saw Fletcher come in with Con Riley. If it was going to spike her guns before she even began to fire them, the sooner Tom and I were seen to be on good terms the better. Only it didn't work out quite like that.

I caught at his sleeve as he passed me and said: 'Tom, come and join us.'

He looked at me absently, as though he scarcely knew me. 'Huh? Oh, it's you. Enjoyed yourself, have you? Nice car, isn't it?'

'Sit down, Tom,' Alan said. 'I'll get you a coffee.'

'Can't stop. Sorry. Just looking for Heathcote.' He walked on down the long room and out at the far door without stopping.

Triss widened her eyes. 'Well! What was all that about? Surely he didn't mind your having driving lessons? He's always said it's best to learn from a professional instructor, hasn't he? . . . Or did they give you a handsome young instructor, is that it?'

'They did not,' I said. 'He was young, yes, but he was spotty and stupid. What's more, he was a darn sight too familiar.' And then, because my eyes were stinging, I got up to go. 'See you,' I said.

Fletcher smiled sweetly as I passed her, and Con Riley said: 'Well, the sweetheart of the forces! I'll say one thing for you, Abby. You don't let the grass grow under your feet, do you, girl?'

'I try not to,' I said. 'How about you?' And then I went up to my room and cried.

CHAPTER FOUR

WHEN Sister Knight took herself off after lunch on Thursday Tom and John Heathcote were still in the ward, Tom filling a request form at the desk, and John writing notes at the other end.

Hearing the double doors flap together as Sister went out Tom looked up quickly at the clock. 'Is it that time already? Good lord!' It was the first time he had addressed me directly since Tuesday, and even now he didn't turn to face me.

'It's half past one,' I confirmed. 'Haven't you had lunch yet?'

'No, and I've got to be away before two.' He pushed his pen back into the breast pocket of his white coat, beside his bleeper, and shoved the signed form across the desk to me as he stood up. 'You might get that sent down to the path. lab., will you?'

I nodded. 'I'll send it as soon as Nurse Phillips gets back, yes.'

'I must fly.' He stood looking at me for a moment, a little uncertainly, and then he added: 'It's Thursday.'

'I know.' I tucked the form behind my apron bib and turned away. 'Enjoy yourself.'

'Yes. I expect I shall, actually. I'm—'

'Sorry,' I interrupted. 'Must rush.' I marched

down the ward to John and left him to see himself out. It wasn't polite, and after all Tom was a registrar, but it was expedient if I wasn't to make a complete fool of myself.

John glanced at my face as he flapped the case-sheets over and hung the clip-board back on its rail over old Mr Turner's dozing head. 'Well,' he said, 'so it's you and me in charge again, is it? At least it isn't our take-in this time, thank heaven.'

'Don't tempt Fate,' I warned him. 'You can't bank on anything in this place. Not since the maestro took over, anyhow. I dare say he's quite capable of sending something in.'

'Not this afternoon, he won't.'

John sounded very sure. 'Oh? Why not? We've got a bed, now that Lambton's gone home against advice.' We had been rather glad to see the back of Mr Lambton, who had fondly imagined that money could buy him more attention than any one patient has a right to expect. He would be back when his renal colic got worse. 'Even Lambton may change his mind.'

'Well, it won't get him anywhere this afternoon. The Master'll be too busy racing that boat of his.'

So he had a boat too? 'Where?'

'Some place called Chasewater, wherever that may be. Well, that's what the man said.'

I was irritated. 'One long round of pleasure, isn't it? What with his E-type, and his boat, and—'

'Oh, well . . .' John shrugged, 'I suppose he's earned it. Roll on my Fellowship!'

'That won't get you anywhere,' I said. 'Look at

Tom. He's got his, and he can't afford boats and whatnot. And if anybody'd love one, he would. He's always—'

'So he was telling me . . . I just want to look at Caldecott again. He's looking better, don't you think?'

'He's fine.' I followed John back along the ward.

'So he'll be in his element, won't he?' he went on, inexplicably. 'Is there a fresh blood-count up?'

'Yes. It's much better.' I leaned across and flipped the form out of the clip for him. 'The haemoglobin's well up, and the reticulocyte count's—'

'OK,' John said maddeningly, 'I can read. I'm not used to being waited on, you know. I'm just a Cas-man at heart. Save it for the big shot. It doesn't impress *me*.'

'It wasn't meant to,' I said crossly. 'I was only—'

'I mean, *I* don't mark the surgery papers. Not a bit of use flapping your lashes at me, is it?'

It was just as well that Nurse Phillips came down to me at that point. When I had sent her off to the path. lab. with Tom's chit I went into the office and stayed there, ruling up the temperature book, until John had gone. I didn't rule it very well, and I had to scrap two pages and do them again.

I was urging the last of the visitors out when the phone rang. Staff Coates, in Casualty, said: 'Can you clear a side-ward, Lake?'

'There's one free,' I told her. 'Our Mr Lambton's discharged himself, or there wouldn't be. Why?'

'Fine,' she said. 'One coming up.'

'It's not our take-in, Staff!' I protested. 'I can't—'

'You'll have to,' she said briskly. 'Head injuries, p.p. All right?' She put down her receiver before I could get another word in.

Phillips and B. J. Williams were out in the ward with the tea-trolley, Peggy Johnston was putting the fresh batch of flowers into vases, and Minnie was on top of a ladder in the linen-room doing something complicated with the spare piles of drawsheets, so it was up to me. I switched on the electric blanket in the side-ward, closed the window and fetched fresh towels, before I told the others we had an admission coming up.

B.J. raised her eyebrows. 'Today? It's not our day.'

'Try telling that to Staff Coates,' I suggested. 'I've seen to the bed and everything, and I'm going to tea now so that I'll be back to cope.'

'Fine,' B.J. said. 'What is it, by the way?'

'Head injuries. Some chap with a motor-bike, I expect. It usually is. Or someone who fell off a scaffold.'

But it wasn't a motor-cycle accident, or a fall at a building site. It wasn't 'some chap' either. When I got back, twenty minutes later, B.J. came trotting out of the side-ward bursting with it, and buttonholed me before I even reached the ward door. 'Didn't they *say* who it was?' she wanted to know. 'Didn't Cas tell you?'

'No.' I frowned at her. 'How d'you mean?'

'Well, I'm sorry to be the one to tell you, old dear, but—it's Tom Fitzgibbon.' She put her hand on my arm. 'It's all right. He'll be OK. Nothing to fash about, Lake.'

'Tom? With *head* injuries?' I cursed all cars and the men who had invented them. 'That damned car, I suppose. He was only saying—'

B.J. was shaking her head. 'No. It wasn't a car-crash. Something to do with a boat, he says.'

'Who says? Tom?' Then at least he was conscious.

'No, of course not. Mr Dell. He's *in* there.'

I pushed past her and walked straight into the sideward. Tom, very white, lay flat without a pillow. There was only a small tuft of hair showing above the bandages. Simon Dell leaned on the foot-rail of the bed watching him. 'What happened?' I demanded, and added: '—sir?'

'A slight argument with a boom, unfortunately. And then with a prop-blade.'

'You mean—you mean Tom went overboard?' It was absurd. Tom wasn't stupid enough to simply fall out of a boat. He looked dreadful too. 'What on earth were you *doing*?'

'Trying to stop the thing capsizing, obviously!'

'But how did he come to go overboard? He's sailed before; he's not a novice. I don't see how—'

'Better ask him,' he said drily. 'He'll be round soon, but he's probably still concussed. I've stitched the gashes up. He ought to be fit enough by tomorrow morning.'

I pulled myself together. Tom was, after all, a patient. 'Yes, sir,' I said formally. 'Have you written him up a sedative?'

'That's Heathcote's job, not mine,' he told me sharply. 'I think you'd better get him. If I'm not capable of stopping idiots from going overboard, I'm evidently not capable of prescribing medication for them either.'

'Tom's *not* an idiot,' I began hotly. But Simon had gone. I heard him walking quickly along the corridor. And then the lift came to rest at our floor, and there were voices, and then a lighter step coming towards me. Sister Knight, I guessed.

She put her head round the door. 'Nurse? What on *earth* have you said to Mr Dell?'

I went over to her. 'I'm sorry, Sister. I'm afraid I did rather speak my mind . . . Was he very angry?'

'Angry?' Her mouth twitched. 'Oh, no, he wasn't angry. He was laughing his head off.'

That exasperated me. 'There's nothing to *laugh* at!'

'No.' She put her head on one side and considered me. 'Now, now, calm down, Nurse Lake. He's quite right—you do look dangerous when you're cross . . . Is Mr Fitzgibbon round?'

'No, Sister. Not yet.'

'Then you just stay with him until he is, hm? And try to simmer down, there's a good girl.'

I was still furious when Tom opened his eyes and looked at me vacantly. Then he closed them again.

'Tom,' I said. 'Tom? Wake up, old love.' Old

love was right, I reflected, as I flicked his cheek with my fingers. 'Open your eyes, Tom.'

He did open them, after a while, but he didn't look very sensible, and after he had stared at me for a full two minutes he frowned and said: 'Go away.' He might have been talking to an over-attentive wasp.

Sister came in a few minutes later. 'Any response yet, Nurse?'

'Not really.' I shook my head. 'I don't think he's orientated, Sister. He doesn't seem to know me, at any rate.'

She walked across to the bed and rubbed his cheek with her knuckles. 'Mr Fitzgibbon! Come along now. Open your eyes. Wake up.'

He evidently saw her as a wasp too. I was glad in a way. It made it less personal. 'Go *away*,' he said for the second time. 'For God's sake . . .' Then he tried to swat her wrist. It was a vicious little movement.

'There's some cerebral irritation there,' she told me, mildly. 'He'd better have his sedative and sleep it off. What did Mr Dell write up?' She reached for the case-notes.

'Nothing,' I said. 'He told me it was the HS's job, as a matter of fact.'

One of her eyebrows lifted. 'He did, did he? Well, I suppose it is, but surely—'

'I did *ask* him,' I stressed.

'Perhaps that was the trouble! . . . All right, we'll get hold of Mr Heathcote.' She looked up at me again. 'He'll be all right, you know. There's nothing to worry about. No fractures or anything.'

'I'm not worried, Sister.'

'No? You should see your face, Nurse. Don't tell me. Run along, and ring the HS, then. And Nurse Williams can take over from you until he settles.'

'But Sister, I—'

'You heard me, Nurse! I won't have people being emotional round my patients.'

I said: 'Very well, Sister,' and went off to the telephone.

It was not until after I had put out a message for John Heathcote that I had time to reflect that she was right. I was worried. And when I found B.J. and told her to go to the side-ward she too looked at me oddly. 'Is he really bad?'

'No. Only a bit off the hooks, that's all. Why?'

'You're a jolly funny colour.'

'Am I? I suppose it was just the shock of finding him here. I'm all right.'

She grinned. 'Love's young dream . . . All right, I'll go to him now. Can you finish this drug cupboard for me? There's only the bottom shelf left to do. It needs sorting out, and I can't be in two places at once. Here are the keys of the castle.'

I pinned the keys to my apron and carried on where she had left off. It was actually my job when Staff Hasan was on duty, but B.J. liked tidying things and she was a confirmed job-poacher. As I worked I went on thinking about Tom's accident. It must have been Simon Dell's fault. It had to be. Tom was capable of high-spirited idiocy at times, but that he could fall out of a boat without some contributory stupidity from someone else I refused to believe. And for the rest of the evening, between helping with beds, giving drugs, and checking dressings, I went on returning to the thought. I was so obsessed with what I saw as Simon's carelessness that I even forgot the vital routine when I went off duty. The junior night nurse came chasing after me to the lift.

'Sister wants you, Nurse,' she puffed apologetically.

I went back to the office. 'Yes, Sister?'

'Where are my keys? Didn't Nurse Williams hand them on to you?' She was frowning at me. 'Do wake up, Nurse!'

'I'm sorry, Sister.' I unpinned them from my bib and handed them over. 'I clean forgot.'

Her look said a good deal.

After that it gave me no pleasure at all to meet Simon Dell along the bottom corridor. I prayed for him not to notice me, but he halted, smiling faintly, and asked: 'How's the patient? Fitzgibbon, I mean.'

I didn't smile back. I was very formal with him. 'I've no idea, sir. I haven't seen him for the last three hours. All I know is—' I realised that I was about to say too much, and stopped.

'Go on.'

He was still, infuriatingly, blocking the corridor and I was beyond the point where I could decide rationally whether or not to give way to my annoyance. 'All I know is that it should never have happened,' I told him abruptly. 'He might have been killed.'

Simon nodded. 'He might indeed,' he agreed. 'He was very lucky.'

I wanted to hit him. 'Lucky? *Lucky?*' I felt as I had when B.J. had told me we were 'lucky' to get Simon in on a Sunday. 'I wouldn't call it luck. It was a matter of sheer incompetence, I should think.'

'Quite,' he said. 'Well, I'm sorry it happened, if you feel so badly about it, Annabel, but—'

'And don't call me Annabel!' I said between my teeth. I pushed past him and tramped on towards the dining room, fuming.

Triss, sitting beside me, watched me leave my shepherd's pie half eaten and said: 'Well? Suppose you tell me what's biting you? I haven't had a civil word out of you yet. Sister Knight been running you around, or what?'

'It's not Sister Knight,' I told her. 'It's that man Dell. He's impossible.'

'Oh? "I do not love thee, Mr Dell"? What has he done now?'

'Nearly killed Tom.'

'You must be joking.' She looked at my face. 'No, you're not, are you? What happened?'

'You mean to say the grape-vine hasn't got hold of it yet?' I found that hard to believe.

'I wouldn't know. I've not been in touch with it since lunch—I've been too busy. We've had three emergencies since three o'clock, and I've been run off my feet. Two of them in hyperglycaemic coma, too. You can imagine. Two of those is a bit much fiddling with drips and all the rest of it. Did they have a scrap? What about? Surely not!'

I explained as well as I could. 'I don't know how it happened,' I added, 'but obviously Mr Dell isn't as good at sailing as he is at surgery.'

'Poor old Tom! Has it really knocked him about a lot, Abby? I mean—'

'Gashed his face and head. And he's concussed, of course. I hope he'll be all right. He didn't even know who I was.' I heard my voice there, because of a break in the chatter around us, and realised that it was practically a wail. 'Sorry,' I said. 'I didn't mean to go on about it.'

Triss was sympathetic. 'It's all right. I know how you must feel, I'd be going dotty if it was Alan. But I suppose it—it takes something like this to make you see how you do feel, doesn't it? You weren't all that sure about Tom, the last time you talked about him, were you? To be honest?'

'I wasn't sure how *he* felt. Changing his half-day and everything.'

'Well, now you see how he meant to spend it. Not with another female at all. At least you've had that much reassurance, haven't you?'

'There's one thing about it,' I calculated. 'Now that the great man's made a stupid mistake perhaps Tom won't be doing quite so much hero-worshipping.'

'Feet of clay? But nobody can be good at *everything*. I think Tom just admires him professionally.'

'To such an extent that he has to spend his

half-day with him? He's behaving like a third-former besotted with the captain of cricket!'

'Miaow!' Triss pushed the milk jug towards me. 'What are men, anyhow? Little boys with money, that's all. Not to worry, Abby . . . Listen, have you heard that the results—the hospital finals—will be out tomorrow?'

'No! Who says so?'

'Miss Black must have told them in the sisters' common-room. Old Haywood's been digging at me all afternoon about it. "If that's the best you can do, my girl, don't expect to see *your* name on that list tomorrow." And so forth. Well, you know what she is.'

I did. 'At least Sister Knight's human. If they'd sent me to Eight I'd have gone raving mad. I don't know how you put up with the woman at all.'

Triss smiled. 'I guess it's just natural resilience, old girl. Wouldn't be a bad idea if you were to cultivate some of that yourself . . . What are you going to do before bed?'

'You'll laugh,' I said. 'There's a jumbo edition of that hospital soap opera on TV. One way of getting away from it all.'

'Too true. All right, I'll join you in the telly room. It'll make a change.'

I didn't really have time to get involved with the Oxbridge gang, because half a dozen of us landed in the TV room while the late news was on the air. We weren't really looking at it but then one of the girls bounced on her chair and burst out: 'Crikey! Isn't that Simple Simon?' and we all sat up to look.

It was Simon Dell, all right: even at an angle of forty-five degrees, taking a smacking racing dive into choppy water, he was recognisable. So was the blood-spattered face on his shoulder as he struggled in the wake of a circling motor launch. 'Lord!' Triss said loudly. 'Abby, did you see that?'

I nodded, speechless.

'He *rescued* him! Did you hear what the man said?'

They all turned to look at me. Somebody at the back said: 'Well, he asked for it.'

I whipped round. It was Fletcher. It would be. I said: 'What do you mean—asked for it?'

'Well, any fool could see they were going to gybe at the marker buoy.' She looked superior. 'Why didn't he duck? He might have known the boom would—'

'Oh, shut up, Fletch,' Triss interrupted. 'I'd like to see you do any better. It was probably the wash from that motor-boat that got them out of control, anyway. You can't blame either of them for that.' She turned to me. 'It was just an accident. It's easily done.'

'He saved him,' I said. 'He *saved* him, Triss. And I was so rude to him. I feel terrible.'

'Well, you can always apologise. Forget it. He's not a fool. He'd know you were wound up.'

After that I couldn't, somehow, concentrate on the TV programme. I was far too busy wondering what to say to Simon Dell when I next encountered him.

I had it all worked out by morning. I would say: 'I'm sorry, sir. I said more than I meant to yesterday. I didn't realise quite what had happened.' And so on. He would be quite within his rights to retort that I hadn't given him a chance to explain, but I should have to weather that. The important thing was to show him that I was sorry, and to thank him for what he had done. As he had said, Tom was lucky. If he hadn't been quick off the mark Tom, unconscious, could have gone down permanently.

We were just finishing breakfast when Miss Crisp came into the dining-room to pin up a list. Molly flapped at once.

'It's the results,' she said. 'I can't bear to look. You tell us, Triss.'

I nudged Triss too. 'Yes, go on. Tell us the worst. I can't bear to look either.'

We watched Triss forcing her way through the tight group that had gathered round the notice-board as soon as Miss Crisp closed the door. She stood there a long time, and when she came back she was wearing her talking-to-patients'-relatives face. My heart sank. 'Well?' we both demanded.

She looked at Molly first. 'You're top in Surgery and Gynae,' she said. 'Well, we guessed you would be. And you're pretty near the top in the other things. I've just about scraped through the lot . . . Abby—'

'Go *on*,' I said.

'Second in Paediatrics.' That was more than I had hoped for. 'Through the other stuff, except—except Surgery.'

'Oh, no!'

'Sorry, old dear. The blighter's failed you.'

'I knew it,' I said. 'I just knew it. Then he'll have failed Con Riley too. He said the same as I did about—'

'No.'

'No? Then who else?'

For once Triss blushed. 'Awfully sorry,' she said. 'You're the only one who's down.'

Molly, bless her, was almost in tears. 'Oh, it *must* be a mistake!' she said at once. 'You can't possibly have failed—it was only that one question you were really worried about, surely? . . . Look, I'll go and ask Miss Black, if you like. She won't mind.'

'No,' I said. 'You're not to. I've got some pride. If I've failed, I've failed, and that's all there is to it. I had a hunch about it all along.' I wanted to cry, I wanted to die, at that moment. I was angry and disappointed together, and if Simon Dell had walked in I might have said a good many things that I'd have been sorry for. As it was I got up quickly from my chair and went straight up to the ward, without even looking at the notice-board for myself. There was no need. Triss didn't make mistakes.

When I'd done my share of the beds Staff Hasan came to me, smiling. 'Have you seen Mr Fitzgibbon yet?' she wanted to know. 'He's fine this morning. Perhaps you'd like to take him his coffee?'

Tom was sitting up. He still had a dazed look, but at least he didn't tell me to go away this time. He didn't even remember saying it the night before, obviously, because he said: 'I wondered when I'd see you, Abby.' Then he looked down at his hands and added: 'I must have had the dickens of a clout from that screw. If it hadn't been for Dell I mightn't, be here.'

That made me impatient. 'If it hadn't been for him it wouldn't have happened at all,' I told him sharply. 'Oh, I know he rescued you—it was in the local news film last night—but it can't have been your fault that you went overboard.'

He laughed and winced together. 'No? It was, though. I just wasn't paying attention, and I didn't get out of the way fast enough. It was just unfortunate that the launch came in close at the same time. Face it, Abby, if Dell hadn't fished me out I'd have been a goner.'

'It was the least he could do,' I said.

Tom frowned painfully, and pushed back the bandage over his eyes. 'He can't do anything to suit you, can he?'

'Not much,' I said. 'And now he's failed me in the surgery paper.'

'That's rough. What went wrong?'

'One bad mistake,' I said. 'That's all. And yet the others who made it are through. Oh, it's not fair, Tom.'

'Doesn't sound like Dell to be unfair,' he said. 'He's so—'

I moved away impatiently. 'That's right, defend him! I might have known you would . . . Is there anything I can get you?'

'A kind word or two wouldn't come amiss!'

'Oh, Tom. You know—'

'I know you're being a silly little girl! Run away, Abby, and calm down.'

He didn't have to tell me twice.

Right outside the door Simon Dell was talking to Staff Hasan, standing there with his back to me, running his fingers through his hair as he nodded down at a treatment sheet she was showing him. He turned to face me as she walked away.

I still don't know what happened in that moment. There I stood, bubbling with all the things I had planned to say to him—about the accident, about Tom, and even, I think, about the exam failure too. And not a word of it would come. He looked me straight in the eyes, and I looked back, and there was a great wall of silence standing there between us. It was he who broke through it, with a quiet: 'Good morning, Annabel.'

Sister Knight saved the situation by emerging from her office while I was still trying to stammer out some kind of answer. It was just as well, because the only thing in my mind as I watched the two of them go into the side-ward was the heroic little picture of Simon flashing into the churning wake of the motor-boat, strong, eager, efficient, and wholly admirable. Just for a second it completely obliterated all the anger and humiliation that had been boiling in my head. It was the oddest feeling.

CHAPTER FIVE

IT WAS a good feeling, but it didn't last. By the time that Molly and Triss had told me several times just how sorry they were about the surgery results, and Sister Knight had said: 'What went wrong, Nurse Lake? I thought you were good at surgery. What got into you?' I was angry again. And after comparing my answers with those the others claimed to have given I was newly convinced that the whole thing was bitterly unfair.

'I suppose he thinks he's been mighty clever,' I grumbled to Triss. 'Falling over backwards to show how jolly impartial he is, after Fletch getting at me about favouritism. But he didn't have to *fail* me, did he? A low pass would have done.'

She nodded thoughtfully. 'So you don't really put it down to that choledochotomy question?'

'Oh, I don't know. I don't know *what* to think. I mean, Con Riley did the wrong op too—*and* he's a hopeless speller—but he passed, didn't he?'

Molly was troubled too, but she said sensibly: 'Well, there's nothing you can do about it, Abby, if you won't go and check with Miss Black. You'll just have to takc it again, I suppose.'

'But when? Suppose they hold me back from the State final on account of it?'

'They won't, if you've got a good enough aggregate,' she said. 'And you must have. The Paediatrics was well over eighty per cent, and that'll help bring it up. Besides, look at Tomlinson, last year: she never did pass her hospital finals, but she got her registration just the same. It just meant she didn't get her hospital cert., or her badge, and she wouldn't get any testimonials.'

'But that didn't matter two hoots to her,' I pointed out. 'She was getting married and packing it in, anyway, wasn't she?'

Triss didn't say anything. She just looked at me, and that didn't help. I went on seething inside all morning. And the angrier I felt with Simon Dell the more attentive I was to Tom. It was childish, and I hardly knew I was doing it until in the end he said: 'Look, Abby, there's no need for all this cherishing. I'm all right. You're going on like a cat with one kitten. It's positively embarrassing. That's the fifth time you've asked me whether I want a drink, you know.'

'I just want you to be comfortable,' I said. 'It's what we're here for, after all.'

'Yes, well, I *am* comfortable, thank you.' He sounded almost exasperated. 'I don't need another drink; my pillows are OK; I'm warm enough; there are no crumbs in the bed; I don't have a headache, and my back doesn't need rubbing. So for Pete's sake buzz off and leave me to myself for five minutes. I never knew you were such a confounded fusspot!'

'I'm not,' I said. 'I'm only—'

He snapped his fingers at me. 'Then trot,' he told me.

Ten minutes later I heard him laughing as I passed his door, and then B.J. came out with his hot bottle ready for filling. 'Not much wrong with *him*,' she declared. 'That crack on the head seems to have cheered him up, if you ask me.'

I sighed. 'Or you have.'

'Oh, come off it, Lake! You're just in a mood because of that wretched exam. Do snap out of it. His Nibs'll be here any minute. He's coming in to see Caldecott again.'

'Then I'm going to early lunch,' I decided.

'You can't. Hasan's going and Sister's down with the engineer having a radiator conference before she goes herself. You'll just have to grin and bear him. Never mind, maybe he'll be late.'

I knew he wouldn't be, and he wasn't. The moment Staff Hasan had picked up her cuffs and hurried down the stairs he got out of the lift with John Heathcote. B.J. vanished into the annexe and left me to it. I said: 'Good morning, sir,' without looking at him, and tried not to feel anything when he answered; and then I stood beside Caldecott and held out the notes for him, and tidied the bed when he had finished. He must have told John to go, because when I followed him through the swing doors we were alone, and he stood looking down at me quietly.

He said: 'You remember what I told you? That I should—'

'Are you going to look at Mr Fitzgibbon?' I interrupted.

'No, I'm not . . . I told you that when the exam results were up I should ask you again to come out with me. Didn't I?'

'Exam results!' I exploded. 'Don't talk to me about the results, Mr Dell. You've—'

'Simon,' he reminded me gently.

I ignored that. 'Haven't you done enough damage? Did you have to take your impartiality so far that it became victimisation? It's *not* fair.'

'What on earth are you talking about?' He roughed up his hair with his right hand and then tried to smooth it down again. '*What* isn't fair?'

He was impossible. 'It isn't fair that I should fail the surgery paper. I had exactly the same answers as other people. A whole lot of us did cholecystectomy—and you can't blame us, when that's what Sir Henry and the others always do.' I could feel the uncontrollable tears of self-pity rising in my eyes, hot and shaming, but I went on talking. 'If that's your idea of fairness, I don't think much of it, that's all.'

'I see. So that's it. Well, now that you've got that off your chest, perhaps we could return to my original question? How about next Tuesday?'

'You must be crazy,' I said. 'I wouldn't go out with you if you were the last man on earth, corny as it may sound. It's true.'

He smiled, a faint infuriating smile. 'No? Well, I'll keep trying. And really, as for that surgery paper of yours—'

'I don't want to discuss it.'

'Just as you like. But if you'd let me explain, Annabel—'

'And don't call me Annabel!' I turned away sharply because I couldn't bear his eyes, and slammed Tom's door behind me.

Tom frowned. 'Now what?' He put down his paperback and waited. 'What are all the raised voices in aid of?'

I let the tears come then. Most of them soaked into the shoulder of Tom's pyjama jacket, but he was very sweet about it, in spite of his surprise, and when I managed to pull myself together he said: 'It's definitely not like you, Abby, to have emotional storms. You're overtired, that's what it is. Can't you get a few days off, lovey, and relax a bit?'

'Of course I can't. I've only just come off study-block. And I'm not overtired. It's just—oh, I don't know. Everything I do and say seems to be wrong. Even you get mad with me—and that man Dell is the absolute end.'

Tom stopped smiling, and the thumb that was smoothing the back of my hand stopped moving. 'What's Dell done to you? Look, but for him—'

'But for him you'd have taken over Sir Henry's job, for one thing.'

'He's a far better surgeon than I shall ever be. And better qualified. *I'm* not complaining. I told you.'

'No, but I am! Do you think *I* like seeing you set aside? I think it's disgraceful, if you want to know.'

Tom took his arm away and pushed me away

from the bed. 'It really doesn't much matter what *you* think, Abby. So don't let's go over all that again. Please.'

'Doesn't it?' I thought of the laughter I had heard, and of B.J.'s pink face as she came out of the side-ward, and said foolishly, spitefully: 'Oh, I realise I'm not B. J. Williams. No doubt what she thinks is of vastly more interest to you. You don't tell *her* to run away and play, I notice.'

'How right you are,' Tom said tightly. 'I don't need to. And if you'd just stop being so damned intense, and be cheerful like her, and develop a bit of perspective—'

It was just unfortunate that Sister Knight, escorting Matron on her rounds, should fling open the door at that point. She didn't say a word then, or after Matron had gone, but when I went to her to report off for lunch she called me into the office and told me to shut the door. I had never seen her so cross before. 'Nurse, I told you yesterday that I wouldn't have anyone being emotional round my patients, didn't I?'

'Yes, Sister.' I wished it didn't take so long for my eyes to get back to normal. 'Yes, you did.'

'And there you are, in Mr Fitzgibbon's room, making a thorough exhibition of yourself. What do you think Matron felt about it?'

'I don't know, Sister.'

'Well, I do! She made herself quite plain to me, I can assure you. And if I hadn't managed to put in a good word for you it might be a good deal more serious. As it is—'

'What did she say, Sister?' I looked up.

'As it is, you're being moved. At once. You can go off straight away and move into night quarters. How we're to manage this afternoon I can't imagine, but there it is.'

'Nights?' I said. I was surprised. 'But it's only—'

'Don't argue, Nurse. It's done. You go to Casualty nights, and Nurse Reid's coming from there and reporting here at five. And please give the keys to Staff Nurse before you go.'

'She has them already,' I said. At least I had done one thing properly. 'And the four-hourlies are all up to date, and I've entered them in the book. There's just Caldecott to turn.'

'Well, Nurse Phillips can do that . . . I'm really sorry to lose you, Nurse, but what else can you expect? We don't ask for miracles; we don't expect a high degree of self-control from new juniors, but I think we can demand it from a nurse whose training is very nearly at an end.'

'I know,' I said. 'And I'm terribly sorry, honestly. But actually it was Mr Dell who upset me, and—'

'Mr Dell! Mr Dell, or Mr Fitzgibbon, or the man who drives the dust-cart, it makes no difference! They're all men. And you seem to think of nothing else lately. If you'd just concentrate on your work for a change you might do better.'

That wasn't fair, either—or I didn't think so at the time—but I said: 'Yes, Sister. I'm sorry, Sister.' There was no point in arguing about it.

*

I didn't go in to night nurses' breakfast. Instead I made myself a cup of tea in the utility room on the night floor. Linda Reid put her head in as I was drinking it. 'Just come to get my gear,' she said. 'Sister Knight sent me off early to change rooms. She's not so bad, is she?'

'She's all right,' I said. 'What's it like in Cas these days? Or rather, these nights? It's ages since I did nights down there. Do I get a junior?'

'You must be joking! No, only a porter to keep hooligans out. It's Joe this week. You never see him half the time. I think he must kip down in the records office or somewhere . . . Mind, if there's a flap on Sister'll send you a runner if you bleat enough about it. It's Saturday—you'll probably need one. I hate Saturdays, after the pubs shut. It's one road-crash after another. Last week I was up to my neck in it. Still, you know it is: you've worked there before.'

'I know,' I said. 'Don't rub it in. Want a cuppa?'

'Thanks . . . And I suppose you've had no sleep?'

'Not much,' I agreed. I shoved her cup over to her and reached for the sugar. 'I dozed for a couple of hours, but I never can get off, first night on. And the next day I've gone past it and I'm too exhausted to sleep. I don't think they ought to shift us from days to nights without a day off in between. How can they expect us to adjust in an hour or two? Why don't they use their brains?'

Reid studied my face. I think she was amused. 'Dear, dear! B.J. *said* you were in a bad mood. Not like you, Lake. What's upset the old applecart?' Then her face was suddenly pink. 'Oh, sorry. I suppose it's that exam paper. Not to worry. I've come down in Medicine. I've had one hell of a ticking off from Miss Black. Let her down, all that.'

'If I'd failed Medicine I could understand it,' I said. 'I even got Addison's disease mixed up with Simmonds', yet they passed me on that. And it was a wicked paper. It just doesn't make sense, does it?'

She wriggled her shoulders. 'Does anything in this dump make sense? Oh, well, we shall soon be out of it. Just the State final, and then you won't see my heels for the dust—*if* I pass the thing. I'm going to join the QAs. Join the Army and see the world, you know. It's a good life, so they tell me. What about you?'

'Me?' It was only a week or so, I reflected, since I'd rejected Miss Appleby's suggestion of a tutorial career; when I'd felt that the whole of my future depended on Tom. Now I was high and dry, with nobody to please but myself. 'Home Sister was egging me on to do Tutorial—but if I can't pass a simple surgery exam what's the use of that? I don't know. Maybe I'll join the QAs too.'

'I've got all the literature, if you're interested. Want to see it?'

'Might as well,' I said.

'I'll shove it in your room. Where are you—fifty-three?'

'Yes, it was the only one empty.'

'I'll chuck it on your bed, then.'

I poured myself another cup of tea, and sat there

drinking it, until it was time to go over to Casualty, and then I went along to my room and put on a clean cap and collected Reid's envelope of papers from the bed. I could go through them before the rush began, I thought.

There was only Staff Coates on duty down there, sitting in the duty-room writing out appointments cards for minor ops. 'I sent Dane off,' she explained. 'There's been nothing doing all evening. You'll be busy later on, I dare say, but if you do have any idle moments you might pack a few dressing drums and get Joe to take them down to CSD, will you?'

'Will do,' I promised. I wondered why Harry Dane couldn't have done them before he went. 'Anything else?'

'Don't think so. Oh, there's an admission coming over from Candley. It's all fixed with One for him to go up, but you'd best get a houseman to admit him—you've got Sister Roe on tonight, and you know what a stickler she is for the red tape.'

'What is it?'

'I don't think they really know. Dr Fisher rang up—said it was a query abdomen of some sort. I suppose he'll be for laparotomy.'

'Right,' I said. 'Have you left me any milk?'

'There's half a pint in the blood fridge, I think. And there's plenty of tea in Sister's cupboard.' She unpinned the keys from her apron bib and passed them over. 'Well, I'll get off. Is there anything decent for supper?'

I had no idea. 'Don't know, Staff. I didn't go to the dining-room. Saturday, it'll be cold anyway. Why they have to send all the maids off on the same night I don't know.'

'Because they're not nurses, Lake. The proles expect their Saturday evenings off come hell or high water. *They* don't know that patients don't take sick by the clock or the calendar, now do they?'

When she had gone I checked the list inside Sister's cupboard to see who was on casualty call. We had no regular Casualty Officer at night: the men worked a rota. Somebody had scribbled out Tom's name and substituted Dr Hai's. That was all right with me. He was a nice little man, even if he did flap sometimes.

He came down as soon as I rang when the yellow Candley ambulance pulled into the park below Casualty windows, and we had the forms filled in no time at all and the man on his way up to the ward. The man was a bad colour, and blank with pain, and after one gentle palpation of his rigid abdomen Dr Hai said: 'Intestinal obstruction, and maybe generalised peritonitis, I think, Nurse. Yes?'

'Looks like it,' I agreed. 'I'll send him straight up, shall I?'

He nodded. 'Someone will have to operate quickly. I must speak with the SSO. Or with Mr Heathcote perhaps?'

'Make it the SSO,' I suggested.

'I shall arrange something at once,' he agreed. 'You will excuse me?'

He was a poppet. 'Come down when you want some tea,' I told him, just to see his wide, eye-obliterating smile. He looked like a very young Pekinese puppy when he did that.

Half an hour later, while I was idly packing drums in the dressing section, I heard someone go into the CO's office, and walked the length of the dark Outpatients hall to see who it was. I reached the yellow slit of light from the door and pushed it open. Simon Dell was in there, bending over the desk to riffle through some papers. He looked magnificent in tails, and I wondered where he had been. And with whom. Without turning his head he said: 'Nurse Reid, didn't they send any notes with this man from Candley? The man Whetton? Hm?' Then he looked up and said: 'Annabel!'

'I've been transferred,' I said quickly. 'No, they didn't . . . sir.'

'They wouldn't! Trust old Fisher to forget . . . So, you're on nights now?'

'Obviously,' I said. I wished he would go away, and stop disturbing me.

He fiddled about with some of the papers, and then tucked them tidily into the corner of the blotter. His hands moved delicately and precisely, I noticed, with great economy of effort. There was nothing untidy about his movements. Watching his fingers made me want to have them touching me too. It was quite illogical, but that was the way I felt and I couldn't find any way of hating him in that moment. I wanted, I know, to move towards him.

Maybe I did just take one step towards the desk. I think I did. And then the telephone shrilled in the duty-room and I turned to run.

It was the police information room. 'Nasty crash at Seven Ways,' the man said. 'Thought you'd like to know. Six hurt. OK? The ambulances won't be long.'

'Thanks for the tip-off,' I said. 'Right—I'll be ready.'

Simon was at my elbow. 'Well?' He had followed me very quietly.

'Just a car-crash coming in,' I told him.

'"Just" a car-crash? Funny word to use, Annabel.'

'You get used to them down here,' I said.

'Do you? *I* never get used to them. We oughtn't to be so acceptant, we ought to—' He stopped. Then he said: 'Sorry. One of my hobbyhorses.'

'One of mine, too,' I said quickly. 'But talking about it doesn't help, does it?' I reached for the telephone again. 'Excuse me—I'll have to get Dr Hai.'

'He's busy with the Candley man. I'm putting him in ice for the time being.'

'You're not going to operate?'

'Not if I can avoid it for a few hours. He isn't fit for that until he's had some blood. I've left Hai to help them—the SSO's out and Heathcote's tied up somewhere.'

'Is that why they fetched you in?'

'I imagine so.' He took off his coat. 'I'd better see these casualties for you, hadn't I?'

'It's not your job,' I said. 'You're a consultant. You're not expected to—'

'I'm a surgeon.'

'Mr Dell—' I began.

'Simon.'

'I'll have to ring Night Sister. She'll be furious if she finds you down here, seeing casualties.'

'Let her be furious,' he said. 'Who's afraid?'

'I am, frankly!'

'All right. To cover yourself, ring her, then. I shall still see the casualties.'

It was a relief when the switchboard man told me that she was busy in the wards. 'Then don't bother her,' I said.

We stood at the window in the half light and waited for the ambulances, listening for their sirens in the distance, and Simon said: 'I'm a glutton for punishment. What *about* next Tuesday?' He put two fingers on my forearm and drew them down slowly to my knuckles. 'Well, Annabel? Would you still not go out with me if I were the last man on earth, as you put it?'

The two fingers slid between three of mine and it was unbearable. 'I don't *know*,' I said despairingly, and pulled my arm away from him. 'Oh, Simon, don't. Leave me alone. It isn't fair of you.'

'You said that before.' He sounded troubled. 'You wouldn't let me explain.'

'Listen,' I told him. 'There's the first ambulance.'

We watched it pull into the park and back up to the reception ramp, and then we walked through to the cubicles. I opened up the first few curtains for the ambulance men and Joe came blinking from his hideout to help with the stretchers.

Four of them, just youngsters, were only shocked, and had glass cuts on their white faces. The fifth, the driver, was in a bad state. He had been thrown out on to the road and one side of his face was scarcely human. One leg lay distorted, drenched with dark blood, and he was crying like an animal. I left Simon with him for a moment and went to the sixth cubicle. The couch was clean and empty. The ambulance driver came across to me, moving his head from side to side. 'B.i.d.,' he said. 'He's out in the ambulance. Maybe the doc will certify?'

'You're sure?'

It was a stupid question, obviously. 'I'm sure,' he said drily. 'You couldn't be the way he is and live, Nurse.'

'If you've got his name would you like to fill in the book for me? Save time. I must go back to Mr Dell.'

By the time I got there he had cleaned up the driver's face. 'Give him a quarter of morphia right away,' he said. 'You recognise him?'

I moved closer and looked down at the pulped cheek and the gravel-rash. It was Call-me-Jeff. Not that he knew me as he stared up blindly at the ceiling. 'It's the driving instructor!'

Simon nodded. 'So much for his own ability.'

'Maybe it wasn't his fault.'

'No? Six people in a Mini? It was his fault all right.'

I nodded, and held up the syringe for him to

check. 'I suppose so.' I shot the stuff into the flac-
cid arm. 'What do you want on that face? Acrifla-
vine?'

'It'll do for now. He'll have to be admitted for
X-rays. If you'll get his clothes off we'll back-splint
that leg. You've got splints?'

'There's plenty of plastic splinting, do-it-yourself
stuff. That do?'

'Anything that'll immobilise it. There's a com-
pound fracture there.'

Joe helped me to cut away Call-me-Jeff's clothes
while Simon looked at the other four. It was easy,
now that he was sedated. I don't think he felt a
thing. His leg was a mess—a tib and fib., and an
oozing hole where his knee should have been, and
great purple bruises from him to ankle.

The others could go home, Simon said when he
came back. 'I've sutured the worst of the cuts,' he
added. 'Told 'em to come up to OP on Thursday.
Now, let's look at this.' He slid his arms into the
gown I was holding for him. 'Thanks. I'd better not
go back to my host looking as though I'd been in a
street fight.'

I tied his tapes. 'Were you at a party?'

'A banquet, no less. Never mind: the important
part was over. I've escaped from a lot of boring
speeches, I expect.'

It took us more than half an hour to clean up
Call-me-Jeff's leg and splint it temporarily, while
Joe fixed a sitting car for the others. When it was
done I said: 'There's another man in the ambulance. A b.i.d. Will you look?'

Simon looked round from the basin where he was scrubbing. 'Seen him yourself?'

'No.'

'You should have done. Never take an ambulance man's word. They're not infallible.'

'They're pretty good.'

'That isn't the point, is it? They're not responsible. Come on. Come down with me.'

I followed him down to the ambulance park and across the gap from the ramp to the open doors. He turned round clumsily. 'I thought you said it was a man. No, don't look. It's not very pretty.'

He wasn't quick enough. I had already seen the child: I had to remind myself that the pathetic sprawling creature had once been a living child, and I felt cold. Simon took one long look and then turned to grasp my elbow. 'Back inside the department,' he urged me. 'March. Sorry, I didn't realise You all right?'

'I'm fine,' I said.

I went on being fine while he filled in forms and talked to the ambulance men; and I cleared all the cubicles and tidied the desk, and filled in the casualty book before I let go. Then I sat down heavily on the chair by the desk. 'That was a bit much,' I said. 'That little boy.'

'So you're not as used to it as you pretend?' Simon was still there, sitting on the windowsill watching me, with his white tie askew and his sleeves rolled to the shoulders. 'Good. Don't *you* grow a shell, Annabel.'

I think that did it. His gentleness, his warm

drawl, and the way he said my name. When he came over to me and took me in his arms I went to him thankfully. I let him kiss me in a sweet sad kind of way that made me want to weep. He was just going to kiss me again, differently, when I thought again about the surgery paper. But I didn't think about it for very long, and if he was aware of my brief hesitation he didn't let it influence him. This time it was strong and reaching, and somehow exultant, and when he took his mouth away we were both a little unsteady. If we hadn't heard Sister Roe's clickety footsteps coming along the passage from the main block there would have been no end to it. As it was, he slid smartly into his coat and out of the office a split second before she arrived.

She looked round suspiciously. 'Finished, Nurse?'

I nodded, and gulped in a deep breath. 'Just, Sister. Five casualties, one admission, and the man from Candley.' I opened the book and went over to wash my hands while she checked. My face was scarlet in the mirror over the basin. 'There was a b.i.d. as well, Sister. A child.'

She made her thin pursed tutting noise and said that really the roads were a death-trap nowadays and why didn't they do something about it. She looked at me as I turned round, drying my hands. 'You don't look too good yourself, Nurse. Are you all right?'

'Yes, thank you, Sister.'

'You don't look it, girl. Your hands are shaking.

Sit down for a minute. You'll have plenty to do before the night's out, I dare say . . . What was Mr Dell doing here?'

'They fetched him to see the Candley admission, Sister, and then he stayed and helped with the casualties. First-On was tied up in Ward One.'

'Huh! Mr Hai. Afraid of his own shadow, that little man.'

I reflected that he was probably terrified of her, but I didn't say so. I turned to drop my towel in the bin. There was a thin gold watch on the shelf above the basin. Simon's. I was amused that he should indulge in that old hospital trick—if it was a trick and not just forgetfulness. I slipped it into my dress pocket and began to pleat a clean towel for the rail. Sister Roe closed the casualty book with a snap and said: 'Well, you don't need me, do you?'

'No,' I told her, 'I don't think so, Sister, thanks.'

'Right. Well, as it's Saturday, I'll see if I can let you have a runner when the wards have settled down. An orderly, at any rate.'

I said: 'Thank you very much, Sister,' and held the door for her.

I stood there holding tightly to Simon's watch in my pocket as she clicked away into the distance. I didn't need her, that was certain. But I knew what I did need, and I had no idea what I was to do about it. It simply wasn't possible that Simon could feel as I felt. It had been just one of those things, where he was concerned, I told myself. I must have stood there for half an hour before I heard the next ambulance pulling in.

John Heathcote came down that time. He was curt with me and impatient with the casualty, and I couldn't help drawing comparisons. Afterwards he said: 'They ought to have their heads examined, some of these kids. Twenty phenobarbs, I ask you.'

I said that I supposed she'd had her reasons. 'Kids of sixteen aren't always blessed with common sense,' I reminded him. 'And she was pregnant, and scared stiff of her people. It could happen to a lot of people.'

'That's what I mean. They just let life do things to them, instead of doing something with life. Idle-mindedness, that's all. No guts, no drive.'

'And maybe nobody to turn to,' I said.

'But people should learn to stand on their own feet. Why should they need "somebody to turn to"? *I* don't need anyone to turn to.'

'Lucky you!' I murmured.

When he had gone I put Simon's watch on my wrist. I wore it all night, except when we had two brawling youths to patch up just before midnight, but he didn't come to fetch it. So it wasn't the old hospital trick, after all. It was just an accident. I didn't know whether to be glad or sorry. I think I was glad, really. At least it meant I could go on telling myself that he wasn't just having fun.

It meant, too, I realised, that I should have to telephone him. It looked a valuable watch: he could be worrying about it, perhaps not remembering where he had left it. I had the sick feeling again when I thought about ringing him. I almost—but not quite—decided to hand it in to the SSO's office for him.

CHAPTER SIX

THE work was practically over before the promised runner arrived. Mrs Skerrett was a fat, breathless, part-time SEN, and how she had ever got through her Roll assessment none of us could imagine. She carried a much-thumbed 1939 edition of a first-aid manual about with her and quoted from it whenever she was corrected. It was her bible. 'The Book says you should use a triangular bandage,' she would insist, just as someone had completed a beautifully precise knee spica, or disapprovingly: 'It isn't like that in the Book.'

The Book was all very fine where simple first-aid was concerned—so long as its perpetual 'hot sweet tea' was kept well away from diabetics—but when I'd worked with her on women's medical she had taken the line that anything that wasn't in the Book in black and white was something the rest of us had invented, and that since it didn't exist she need do nothing about it. So she spent all her time commiserating with the patients while we did her work as well as our own. And because she was old enough to be our mother she got away with a good deal of assumed authority.

She said: 'Oh, so it's *you* down here, is it?' when she arrived. She dumped her great shapeless roll of putty-coloured knitting on the desk and took her battered red Thermos from under her arm, and looked round frowning. 'I *thought* it couldn't be Nurse Reid. Not with Sister's curtains all higgledy-piggledy like that.' She went over and twitched them about an inch, and then turned to inspect me. She noticed the watch straight away. 'Better not let Night Sister see you wearing that watch on duty,' she told me. 'You know we're not supposed to wear wrist-watches, not in uniform.'

'I know,' I said. 'Will you get those drums down to CSD for me? You can take them on the trolley.'

She sniffed. 'I thought the porter was supposed to—'

'Joe's busy,' I said untruthfully. If I knew him he was just settling down to his second beauty sleep somewhere in the dark rooms round the waiting hall, and I felt Mrs Skerrett needed occupation. 'If you'll just—'

'Gold, is it?'

I blinked at her. 'Gold?'

'The watch.' She jerked her head at it. 'Gold, isn't it?'

'Oh, that . . . Mrs Skerrett, don't forget the little glove drum too, will you?' I took the watch off again as I walked out and pushed it into my dress pocket. Maybe she would stop talking about it if she couldn't see it.

It worked. When she came back lugging the empty trolley she said: 'That stock cupboard's a sight. Good mind to tidy it while I'm here. Can I have Sister's keys to get some more wool?'

I looked up from the desk. 'The cupboard isn't locked.'

'Not *locked*? Well! I don't know what Sister Davies'd say, I'm sure.'

I sighed. 'Who on earth do you think is likely to come down here stealing that sort of stuff? Wool and gauze and bandages? It's not as though there were any drugs in there after all . . . Tell me how many rolls you take.'

'People'd steal anything. Anything. They'd have the gold out of your teeth, some of 'em. I know. If you'd been here as long as I have, Nurse Lake, you'd be a bit more careful. Why, they even—'

The telephone rang again then. I was glad of the interruption. It was only the ward nurse wanting some details of the Candley man's home address, but I managed to spin out the conversation until Mrs Skerrett had gone off with her four blue rolls of cottonwool. After that I made myself very busy checking off the written-for minor ops for next day, so that I could see that the right number of beds was ready in the rest-ward. I could well understand Matron's obsession with lists: ticking off names is a restful occupation which looks important and concentrated and allows free rein for undercover thought. And I had plenty to think about.

After morning dinner I sat on my bed for more than an hour in a cold night-duty daze before I dared ring Simon's home number. One didn't disturb consultants first thing on a Sunday morning, I imagined, and it was well after ten o'clock when I went along to the booth on the night corridor. There was no reply. I tried again twice during the next hour without result, and then I wrote a note instead and went down to put it in his pigeonhole. After that I fell into bed, nearly asleep on my feet.

Sister Davies was on duty that night when I got down to Casualty. She didn't look pleased. She said: 'Ah, you're here, Nurse Lake. I want a word with you in my office, please . . . Close the door, Nurse . . . Now, you were on duty down here last night, I believe?'

I suppressed a convulsive yawn, widened my eyes, and tried to concentrate. 'Yes, Sister.' I wished I could go back to bed. 'Anything wrong?'

'Mr Dell's been down. He says he left his watch behind last night, and he's pretty sure he left it here in Casualty. At any rate, the theatre people haven't seen it. Well?'

I was fully awake now, and I didn't like her accusing tone. 'Yes, he did, Sister.'

'Then where is it? What have you done with it?'

'It's here,' I said. Only it wasn't. I left my hand in my pocket and thought back quickly. When had I taken it off? And where was it now? 'Oh, it's in my room, I think.'

'You *think*! Oh, really, Nurse, it's too bad! You—'

'Well, I thought I'd better take charge of it, Sister. And I did try to ring him, only I couldn't get any reply.'

'So you simply did nothing about it?'

'No, I—' Students, I reflected, did not write notes to consultants. Not in Sister Davies's book. 'I did leave a message for him.'

'Did you, indeed? Then he obviously didn't get it. Is the watch *safe*, Nurse?'

'Of course. My room's locked, Sister.'

She breathed out exasperation. 'Well, I can't stay here while you go and get it. You'll just have to make your own peace with Mr Dell if he telephones. Why on earth you didn't hand it in to Night Sister I can't imagine. You'd no *right* to keep it in your possession at all. I do wish you would use a bit of common sense, Nurse Lake! No wonder you came down to us with an unsatisfactory report.' She dropped the keys on the desk noisily. 'There you are. And try not to lose those. I hear you were careless with the keys on Ward Three.' She pulled her cuffs on and rustled out. I head the *clip-clop* of her flat heavy shoes, like a horse at the walk, fading away down the long corridor until it was obliterated by the traffic sounds outside.

I answered the telephone three times before ten o'clock, each time trembling a little in case I should hear Simon's voice. Then I had a little spate of minor casualties—a hand crushed by a window-sash, an epileptic lad brought in from the street outside, a blind man who had been jostled by youths and fallen heavily in the gutter. Then a talkative mother brought in a young girl with a violent epistaxis.

I plugged the girl's nose with adrenalin gauze and sat her upright in a straight chair, drinking iced water. Her mother said: '*We* always lay her down when she has these nose bleeds.' She sounded exactly like Mrs Skerrett. 'Always lay her down, we do.'

'Then you shouldn't,' I said sharply. 'How often does she have them?'

'Oh, all the time. Well, once or twice a week, like.'

'And you've not seen a doctor?'

'What? Just for nose-bleeds? 'Course not. It's girl-like, isn't it?'

I enlightened her, and added: 'You'd better bring her up in the daytime, and make an appointment to see someone in the ENT clinic. She's very likely got a thin vessel or a polypus that needs cauterising. She can't keep losing blood like this.'

'Oh, I don't know. Nature's safety-value, they say, don't they? A good old nose-bleed. Clears the head.'

She out-Skerretted Skerrett, I reflected. 'Rubbish! Maybe in a middle-aged person with high blood pressure, yes. Not in a child of her age. She'll be thoroughly anaemic soon if this goes on.'

'Yes, that's what the school nurse said. That she was anaemic, like.'

'But you've done nothing about it?'

'I told you, no. Anaemic, that's not a disease, it's how you are. Some are, some aren't. It's your nature to be pale or it isn't. She's always—'

The telephone rang while she was still rambling on. I was furious and the caller got the brunt of it. 'Well?' I said. 'Casualty, what is it?'

'Nurse Lake?' Simon. It would be.

'Yes, speaking.' I tried to wind down. 'Who is it?'

'Ah, Annabel. You're busy, I take it? You sound it.'

'No, not really. I'm sorry. It was—'

'I won't keep you. Did you find my watch?'

'Yes. Didn't you get my note?'

He was silent for a second, and I heard paper rustling at the other end. Then he said: 'I see . . . Yes, I did.' I got the impression he had only just opened it. 'Good. I wouldn't want to lose it. It was—it was a present. Look, I can't get over for it tonight. Could I see you in the morning?'

'Of course,' I agreed. 'Where will you be?' If he had rounds, I calculated, I could catch him on his way in.

'I'll be free until two. Suppose we meet for coffee, about eleven, and you bring it with you, hm?'

'Yes, I—' I stopped. Hadn't I said I wouldn't go out with him, not if he was the last man on earth? But then this was different. It wasn't an outing for pleasure, it was business.

'Well?' he was saying. 'Where shall I see you?'

I collected myself and tried to sound business-like. 'I'll be in the public library at eleven. I want to call there.'

That amused him, for some reason. I could hear the unevenness of his breathing. 'Good enough,' he said. 'I'll pick you up from there.' I heard the receiver go down.

The epistaxis seemed to be under control when I

turned back to the chair. 'That's fine,' I heard myself saying kindly. 'Just sit still for a few minutes, dear, so that we can be sure it's stopped . . . Would you like a cup of tea, Mother?'

'I don't mind if I do, I'm sure.' The mother looked baffled, and I was hardly surprised. 'And I'm sorry if I give any trouble, Miss. Nurse, I mean. You know best, I'm sure. Only we're used to Sandra here, see, and—'

'I know.' I even smiled at her. 'But you see it can be cured so easily that it's a pity not to have it done. So do make an appointment, won't you? Say you'd like to see the Casualty Officer, and he'll send you on . . . I'll go and make that pot of tea.'

Joe was ahead of me. He was warming the pot conscientiously. 'Here every other night, that one,' he told me gloomily. 'I thought it'd mean a cuppa before we'd done. Don't know how you got the patience, straight up. Want shooting, some of 'em.'

Mrs Skerrett arrived at twelve. 'Supposed to relieve you for Meal,' she announced. 'That's if you want to go, of course. I can tell you it's only lamb curry and apricots, so please yourself. Anyhow, they don't need me upstairs till after two.' She was wearing an odd expression that I didn't understand. 'Or did you want me for anything else?'

Curry would be just fine, I said, reaching for my cuffs. Only I didn't go up to the dining-room. I felt the same about lamb curry and tinned fruit as she did, and I had more important things to do. I went over to night quarters.

Simon's watch wasn't on my dressing table, where I expected to find it. It wasn't in the pocket of the dress I'd put to go to the laundry. It wasn't in my room at all. I even looked under my pillow and in my dressing gown pockets and my handkerchief drawer. I'd been so sleepy that I might have put it almost anywhere. There's not much in a hospital bedroom, and when I'd searched it three times from top to bottom in twenty minutes I was quite sure the watch wasn't there. I sat on the edge of the bed, trying to remember. I'd taken it off, I knew that, and put it in my pocket. I remembered the smooth feel of it in my hand when I'd been talking to Mrs Skerrett. I was still wearing the same dress, and I still had the same box of matches, the same chain of safety-pins and the same notebook. But the watch wasn't there. I began to panic, and went racing back to Casualty.

Mrs Skerrett eyed me strangely, as she'd done when she came on. 'Been meaning to ask you,' she said heavily. 'You lost anything?'

'Why?'

'You look as if you'd lost a bob and found a tanner,' she told me. 'That's why. *And* because there's some careless people about. I thought I'd keep my mouth shut, for a bit. See if you asked. Teach you a lesson.' She smirked complacently.

I began to frown. 'What are you talking about?'

'Well, what do you *think* I'm talking about?' She ferreted in her bulging knitting bag. 'Missed this then, have you?' She dangled the watch in front of my nose and my diaphragm lurched. 'That what you're looking for?'

'So *you've* got it! I do think you might have—'

'Teach you a lesson, like I said. Leaving a valuable thing like that about. Good thing I'm honest, isn't it?'

I took it angrily. 'Where did you get it?'

'Off the desk, of course, where you left it.'

I remembered then. I'd had it in front of me, watching the time, as I waited for Staff Coates to come on duty, and Joe had fetched me away to get him some stomach powder and I hadn't gone back. So that was it. I supposed I ought to be grateful, but I only felt annoyed with Mrs Skerrett. 'Thank you,' I said as evenly as I could. 'But I was worried sick when I couldn't find it. I do think you might have told me sooner.'

'Yes, well, you'll be more careful another time, won't you?'

I said I certainly should, and sent her off to her own meal.

I was beginning the crossword in the *Guardian* when Simon tapped me on the shoulder in the reading room. 'Sorry, Annabel,' he said. 'I'm a bit late. Come on—we'll go to the Grand for some coffee. Unless you'd like to go somewhere else?'

It wasn't the time or place to argue: the old men with their racing editions were already looking at us and muttering. I walked beside Simon the fifty yards to the Grand Hotel and sat beside him on the banquette at the corner table. Then I said: 'Here's your watch, Simon. Have it now, before I lose it.' I took it off my wrist and passed it to him. 'I did try to telephone you, as a matter of fact, but there was no reply.'

'On Sunday? No, there wouldn't be.' He signalled the waiter and held up two fingers. 'I'm not often at home then.'

'So I gather.' I remembered the Sunday we'd sent for him to Ward 3. 'Golf, I suppose?'

'Golf?' His eyebrows went up. 'Hardly.'

'Sailing, then.'

'Not sailing, either. No, I have a duty visit most weeks.' He looked withdrawn, and I wondered why. 'Thanks for looking after the watch. It was a present . . . From my wife, as a matter of fact, shortly before she died. I'm sure you understand.'

'Yes,' I said, 'I understand.'

He leaned back while the waiter set down the tray. 'Will you pour, Annabel? . . . Black, please . . . I was worried when I came down and nobody knew anything.'

'But you got my note. You said so,' I pointed out.

'Ah, yes. Your note . . .' He put two lumps of sugar into his coffee and fiddled about with them, rescuing them and then leaving them to drown. 'I did get it. Only I couldn't read it.'

'You couldn't *read* it?'

He shook his head. 'That handwriting of yours really is a menace. It looks so pretty—but it's illegible half the time. Especially when you're in a hurry.'

I was indignant. 'Other people can read it!'

'Sure?'

'Well . . .' I thought of Molly and Triss. 'Yes, now and again people have found it difficult, I suppose.'

'What are you going to do about it, Annabel?'

'I do try to write clearly. Only when I hurry—'

'Such as when you took the surgery exam?'

I stared at him. 'Are you—You're not saying *that* was illegible?'

'A lot of it was, I'm afraid.'

I put my cup down quickly. 'Look, are you saying that that's why I was failed? Because if so—'

'That's exactly what I *am* saying. Heaven knows you may have had all the right answers, but if they couldn't be read, what good were they?'

I was angry with myself as much as with him. 'Well, I think that's most unfair.'

'Do you?' He stopped stirring his coffee and set the spoon down very gently in the saucer and went on looking at it. 'Look at it like this—it's a thing that could be dangerous. Just suppose that through your writing a patient got the wrong medication, something positively dangerous to him. Or something went to the wrong patient. Things like that. You do see the point?'

'Some of the housemen have disgraceful writing,' I said defensively.

'That doesn't let you out, Annabel. Besides, what about your State final? That's important to you, isn't it?'

I felt about six. 'Yes,' I said at last 'You know it is.'

'So we have to do something about it. Right?'

'We?'

'We. Maybe I can help. I've had the same problem myself, in the past.'

'But your writing's so clear.'

'Is it?' He smiled. 'It used not to be. And it wasn't until *I* failed an exam through it that I pulled myself together and set out to learn all over again . . . Annabel, I'd like to help you, if you'll let me.'

That was really rather funny. 'Help me? After failing me in the surgery paper?'

'But I didn't. *I* didn't mark the papers. Sir Henry said he'd promised to do them, and do them he did. I had nothing to do with it. Even if I'd been asked I wouldn't have done, not once I'd found out that you were up for it.' He leaned over to refill my cup. 'After what you said about somebody or other thinking you might be currying favour, that day we went to the Willow Tree.'

'And I've been blaming you,' I said feebly. 'I thought it was because of the choledochotomy question.'

'Little idiot. I wouldn't have failed you on that, anyway, if you'd shown clearly that you knew the operation you were accustomed to. The fact that it wasn't my pet method would have made no difference. Give me credit for some sense!'

I felt shaken, and it seemed to me that I must be showing it, too, because after a moment or two he said: 'Move round the corner, Annabel, you'll be nearer to the radiator. You look cold.'

I moved along the bench and he shifted the table

and sat down beside me. Then I said: 'I've been an idiot of the first water, haven't I?'

'You have, rather. Never mind, I have a plan.'

'What sort of a plan?'

'About your writing, I mean.'

'Oh, that.'

'Yes, *that*. It's important.'

I sighed. 'Well, what do I do? There isn't a lot of time before the State, you know.'

'I know. First I'm going to lend you a book. It's called *Sweet Roman Hand*, and—'

'Oh, lord, all that italic stuff?'

'That's right. All that italic stuff. And you're going to read it, and copy from it, every day. You've plenty of time as long as you stay in Casualty. It's quite quiet down there after midnight, if it's like any other Casualty department I've ever known. Isn't it?'

'Often, yes. Not always.'

'Often enough. And to make it practical, every day you're going to write me a short note, legibly, to practise the script. You'll be slow at first, but you'll be surprised how soon you'll speed up.'

'Write to *you*?' I couldn't believe my ears. 'But you won't have time to—'

'I'll make time.'

'Why should you?'

He smiled sweetly, and I felt my legs turning to cottonwool all over again. 'Let's say that I see it as important remedial work that has to be done. Will you co-operate?'

I nodded. 'I'll try.'

'Good.' Somehow he had picked up one of my hands, and he was holding it tightly. 'You're a very sweet girl, Annabel, but I'm not blind to your faults.'

I wanted to say that I wasn't blind to his, either, but somehow I couldn't find the words. All I could get out was: 'It's time we went. If we're not in bed by twelve there are ructions.'

He stood up at once. 'We can't have that. I'll run you back straight away.' He left money on the coffee tray, and pulled out my chair as I got up. 'Come on. We'll go through the side door. The car's just outside in the alleyway.'

If I had walked straight out and not looked back I shouldn't have seen them. But I'm naturally clumsy, I suppose. At all events I caught my heel in the mat near the door, half tripped, and turned as I recovered my balance. In the car I said: 'That was very tactful of you, but you needn't have bothered, Simon.'

'What was?' He manoeuvred the E-type out into the main road traffic and glanced at me quickly. 'What was tactful?'

'Getting me to sit nearer to the radiator, and then come out at the side door. You didn't want me to see Tom Fitzgibbon, did you?'

'Guilty,' he admitted. 'Didn't seem much point in harrowing you. Who was she? I know her face.'

'Williams,' I said. 'B. J. Williams. She's on Three. To tell you the truth I'm not surprised.'

'Then I apologise.'

The traffic was fairly sticky after that, and we

didn't talk until he had dropped me fifty yards from the Home. He had wanted to take me right to the door, but I had more sense than that. When a car draws up there, there are plenty of inquisitive eyes at the bedroom windows, to say nothing of Home Sister's look-out point.

He leaned across me to open the low door and said: 'Then tonight you'll write to me, and put it in my pigeonhole?'

'I'd better see this book first, hadn't I?'

'I'm going home to get it now, and I'll leave it for you. You'll have it when you go on duty.'

I was horrified. 'Don't for heaven's sake leave it with Sister Davies! I'm in bad books already, over your watch. Leave it in the porter's hutch.'

'That's what I meant to do.'

'She thinks I'm totally irresponsible as it is. And if she thought I was—well, *hobnobbing* with you, as she'd put it—'

'And aren't you?'

'No.'

He leaned closer. 'Annabel, look at me.'

I walked right into that one with my eyes open. As I turned my head he kissed me quickly on the lips and straightened up again. I could only pray that nobody had seen. 'Now, are you hobnobbing with me?'

I got out of the car quickly and closed the door, and from that safe distance said: 'No. You're giving me writing lessons, that's all.'

'That will do very well for a beginning.' He was laughing as he drove away.

Half way up to the night floor there were half a dozen day nurses milling about in their dressing gowns. Triss was one of them. She wasn't due on until one o'clock, she said, so I took her up to my room. She sat cross-legged on the end of my bed and said: 'Go ahead. I can see you're bursting with something. I'm a natural born listener.'

The funny thing was that when I got into my own dressing gown, and squatted at the other end of the bed, I couldn't tell her a thing. Not about Simon, or the exam papers, at any rate. It just wouldn't come out. So I told her about seeing B.J. with Tom instead.

'But I thought he was off sick,' she said.

I nodded. 'He is—that's why he was out at that hour. He can't go on the wards with his face covered in strapping, can he? Anyway, that isn't the point, is it? It's B.J. That's the thing. I never thought—'

'Nor did I,' Triss mused. 'When has she ever bothered with him before? I thought she had a little friend in the Path. Lab., to be honest.'

'Well, she was there with Tom.'

Triss looked up at me. 'What were *you* doing there? It's a bit pricey for coffee, isn't it? Or was someone else paying?'

'Who, for example? . . . Do you think he's keen?'

'How do I know? Look, you used to think he was sweet on Sister Pleydell. Now you think it's B.J. If you ask me, Tom's just as interested in you as he is in anyone, but if he was honest he'd tell you that his work means more to him than the girls. That's what you're really up against, you know. Wedded to his blessed profession, same like you said yourself. What's B.J. got that you haven't?'

'Legible handwriting, maybe,' I said.

She grinned. 'Well, yes, there is that. Yours is pretty awful. It always has been.'

'Now you tell me,' I said. 'You might have told me so a bit more firmly before the exams.'

'You think that's what failed you?'

'Could be,' I said. 'By the way, it was Sir Henry who marked the papers, after all.'

'I know *that*. Miss Black said so.'

'Well, you might have told *me*. When you're on nights nobody tells you anything.'

'I thought I had. Anyway, you can't say it was the abominable Dell man who ploughed you in surgery, can you?'

I resisted the temptation to say that he wasn't abominable at all, and got to my feet. 'If I don't get to bed I shall be dead tonight.'

At the door Triss looked back. 'I don't know why you didn't come clean. All this guff about B.J. and Tom. Willis saw you through the end window, and so did Tonkin.' Then she closed the door.

I didn't unwrap the parcel I'd picked up at the lodge until Staff Coates had gone and I had the department to myself. There were two books, in fact. One of them was *Sweet Roman Hand*, and the fly-leaf was inscribed: *All my love to Simon—Jean*, in beautiful script done with a broad pen and Indian ink. The other—*Calligraphy for Today*—had a child's pencil scrawl in the front that said: *For Dada from me.*

I looked at those fly-leaves for a long time. Was this whole thing a way of telling me? I'd known about his wife in any case, since the day I'd had that first driving lesson—except that I hadn't known her name. Now it seemed there was a child as well. Was it a boy, or a girl, I wondered? Who was 'me'? Not very old, I guessed: the printing date was only three years back. And was that his Sunday 'duty visit'? To his son—or his daughter?

I was glad when an ambulance pulled in, and I could occupy myself in ringing for the SSO to come down and set a Colles' fracture for an old lady who'd slipped on a piece of soap as she got out of the bath.

He brought Tom, strapping and all, into the plaster room with him. 'Don't let this young man's face bother you,' he told the old lady. 'He's had an accident himself, but it won't stop him giving you a nice anaesthetic while we make your hand comfortable.'

The old lady, whose relatives had already given her several aspirins, giggled, and when I told Tom she'd already been well sedated and wouldn't need much, she said: 'Ay, and I had a nice drop of brandy, too. Took the pain out all right.'

'Then you don't need me, Mother,' Tom told her. 'Just a little whiff, that's all you'll get.' Unacountably he put his hand down hard over mine as I brought up the trolley. It was an oddly familiar warmth. It was deliberate, too, because he murmured: 'I want to talk to you afterwards.'

Maybe he did intend to, but in fact, once the wrist was finished, he was called away with the SSO to deal with a cut-down in Ward One. I wondered whether it was Call-me-Jeff who needed them, and that reminded me of the broken child, like a broken doll, lying in the ambulance when Simon and I had gone down to make sure. If he had a child of his own it was not surprising that he had been so affected.

Sister Roe put her head in once, just to say that as the wards were busy and I wasn't she wouldn't be sending Mrs Skerrett. I should have to leave Joe when I went to Meal, and he could ring the dining-room if anyone needed me. After that it was pretty quiet, and I got out Simon's books and began idly doodling one of the alphabets on the backs of old appointment cards that Sister Davies used for scrap. Then I got on to whole words. They were legible, but they didn't look right. Next morning, I promised myself, I would go out and buy a proper broad-nibbed pen.

I went to Meal, somehow got through a cold tough omelette and a helping of overcooked plums that had nearly become jam, and went back to my practising. At two o'clock Joe called me to a cup of tea in the duty-room. 'Meant to tell you,' he said. 'Mr Fitz come looking for you when you was at Meal.'

'Oh? What did he say?'

'Never said nothing. Went in the office looking

for you, come out again, said where was you, and off. "Any message?" I said. "No," he said, "just tell her it don't matter." That's all he said, Nurse.'

I shrugged. 'Can't have been anything very important, then, can it?' I took my tea back to the office with me, and left Joe to his greasy packet of sandwiches. I would learn to write legibly if it was the last thing I did. And there was that note to write to Simon, too. It would have to be a very short one.

CHAPTER SEVEN

LOOKING after keys is instinctive in hospital, and
though I'd twice been accused of carelessness I was
just as drilled in the routine as anyone else. So I
ought to have known at once what had happened,
because the bunch of bright keys, with its red tag,
that had been lying on the desk in front of me a
second before the heavy brass inkstand crashed
upwards into my face, was no longer there when I
opened my eyes.

There was salty blood in my mouth and the back
of my neck was a wedge of excruciating pain. My
cap, I could see without moving, was over on the far
corner of the desk, rocking a little as I breathed, a
white bowl on the big casualty book. When I
pushed with my hands to lever myself upright it
overbalanced and fluttered to the floor. Then,
seeing dark blood on the blotter, I knew. It had
happened only a month before at the General and
we had all said: 'It can't happen here,' as people do.
And now it had.

I crouched there, quite still, and listened. All I
could hear was the *bleep-bleep* of the dripping tap
in the first cubicle. I got up very carefully so that my
head wouldn't fall off—or that was how it felt—and
mopped my mouth tenderly with a square of gauze
from the box by the spatula jar before I picked up

the telephone. My voice was oddly gruff, and my lips were stiff, and all I managed to get out was: 'A resident, quickly,' and then I let the receiver fall. It took me several seconds to pull it up on its cord and replace it, and then I walked unsteadily into Sister's room.

There was no mistake. The keys were still dangling in the wide-open door of the drug cupboard. There were three green Desbutal capsules lying on the floor, and an empty pillbox crunched under my foot. Everything had gone, even the boxed sprays of local anaesthetics. I found the drug-book fallen under the radiator and tried to check, but I was too muddled. I only knew that everything had gone—morphia, pethidine, scopolamine, atropine, heroin, coramine, everything. I was still trying to add up the quantities when Dr Hai came trotting in. And then, because there was someone else to take charge, I suppose I must have passed out.

When I surfaced again I was in bed—Ward 6's sideward at a guess, because nobody but Sister Cracken would have put up with such dingy old green curtains—and Tom and Sister Roe were standing at the foot of the bed watching me. Sister Roe moved alongside as I opened my eyes and said: 'About time, too!'

I blinked up at her through the wisp of hair across my eyes, and then I looked at Tom. 'Somebody—somebody hit me,' I said. My mouth was still stiff, and it came out thickly. 'They took the DDA stuff.'

'Yes, we know.' Tom nodded, and the light

glistened on the strip of pink strapping along his cheek. 'See anyone?'

It hurt too much, shaking my head, and I gave up the attempt. 'No.'

'Hear anything?'

I closed my eyes to think. 'No. Not after I left Joe.'

'What time was that?'

'Twoish, I think. Yes, it was.'

'It was nearly four when you rang through.'

'Doesn't Joe—Didn't Joe hear anything?'

Tom smiled faintly. 'He says he was cleaning up the orthoptic clinic from two-thirty onwards, up at the far end.'

'Nurse—' Sister Roe was breathing heavily with impatience and I could tell she was angry. 'Nurse, were you *asleep*?' she asked sharply.

'Of course not, Sister.' I moved my eyes but not my head and I could see the irritable flush on her cheeks. 'No, I wasn't.'

'Well, I really fail to understand how—'

'Leave it, Sister.' Tom came to the other side of the bed and gently pushed back the hair that was blocking my view. 'All right, Abby. You get some sleep in . . . Head painful?'

'Neck,' I said. 'And mouth.'

'Yes. You must have gone down on the inkstand pretty hard. You managed to jam the lid. Forget it now. I'm going to give you a shot, so that you can sleep it off.'

'What about that policeman?' Sister Roe asked impatiently. 'You told him to wait.'

'I know I did.' Tom slid a needle into my forearm so that I hardly felt it, and then rubbed the spot meditatively with the cold swab. 'And I'm going to tell him now to come back later on.'

'But he says—'

'Let him say.' He winked at me—it was like old times—and put my hand back under the bed-clothes. 'I'm the doctor.'

'You shouldn't be on duty at all.' Sister Roe sniffed, jerked the sheet across and tucked it in viciously. 'Well, I suppose you know what you're doing.'

'Yes, Sister,' Tom said. 'Sleep now, Abby.'

I slept.

They sent a policewoman to see me at ten o'clock. She was very pretty, which surprised me somehow, with a fair fluff of hair curling up behind her awful cap, and I told her as much as I could. It wasn't much. Then she went away and Sister Cracken came lumbering in with her own best morning tea service, the Poole pottery she thought so much of, and said: 'Now, my dear, how about a nice cup of tea? I'll have mine with you, shall I?'

She was a motherly old thing, and hers was the slackest ward in the hospital. If it hadn't been for Staff Bergen, who was a Danish twelve-month exchange type, the ward would have run down into complete stasis. All the same, she was a very good nurse of the old school: she made the patients feel comfortable, and that was something. I couldn't imagine how she got on with her consultant, Mr

Frigate—'Sailor' we called him—because he was one of the terse fortyish efficiency boys with unbounded energy and very little patience.

I began to reorientate then. I said: 'Did anyone bring up my things from Cas? All my books and stuff, and my cape?'

'They're in my office, dear, yes. I'll get them for you when I go through. Well, what a thing to happen! Teenagers, I suppose. Terrible, the way they're using drugs, isn't it?'

'Not just teenagers,' I said. 'The twenties are worse, from what I hear. They must be terribly unhappy.'

'Why do they *do* it? You're young, Nurse Lake, and you don't. I don't think we've ever had a case of a nurse who—No, I'm wrong. We did, once. But it was very sad, really. Her fiancé was killed, you know, in an accident. Well, he died when they brought him in. And she just happened to be relieving in Casualty that night. It must have been a quite dreadful shock . . .'

I tried to put myself in Harrison's place—I knew it was Harrison, because she had been a legend when I joined—and failed.

'And she couldn't forget it, you know,' Sister Cracken was rambling on. 'Nembutal, it was, with her. To begin with. She couldn't sleep, you see. And then she took an overdose. If it hadn't been for Night Sister—Sister Pettifer it was, at the time—going to her room to alter her nights off in a hurry, she'd probably have died . . . Of course, she had to go. Matron wouldn't keep her after that.'

I was beginning to feel drowsy, listening to the slow old voice. 'What happened to her in the end, Sister?'

'I don't know, Nurse, not to be sure. But I did hear she was married, so all's well that ends well, isn't it? Another cup, now? No? Then you must have a little nap.'

I said: 'When can I get up, Sister?'

'Not till Miss Meadows says so. You were asleep when she did her round, but I expect she'll be up later in the day. You rest while you can, my dear, and think yourself lucky.' She bustled out with the tray, and then fixed a door-handle sausage of red serge to stop it banging. She was full of those old-world tricks.

After a while the junior came in with my night bag. She was all eyes. 'Poor Nurse Lake!' she said reverently. She was just out of PTS, I think. 'Do you feel terrible? I've brought your things. Oh, and there were a couple of notes for you in the ward pigeonhole.' She fished them out from behind her apron bib. 'I'll just leave them on the locker, shall I?'

When she had tiptoed out I reached for them sleepily. The first was from Triss and Molly, a joint effort. They'd heard all about it at breakfast, they said, and they were sorry, and did I need anything brought over from the Home? The other was in Simon's warm square script. It was very short. *My dear Annabel, you know how sorry I am about this—or you ought to. What bad luck. I'll try to come up and see you this afternoon if I get half a chance. Meanwhile, my love to you. Simon.*

Staff Bergen ushered him in, very formally, at three o'clock, after Sister had gone off, and when he said he didn't need her she clearly thought it most unorthodox and compromised by leaving the door wide open. Simon went over and closed it, and then came back and kissed my cheek very gently. 'The rest of you looks too painful,' he apologised. 'How do you feel?'

'A bit woozy,' I said. 'Simon, who's "me"?'

He was puzzled. ' "Me"?' He tilted his head to one side. 'How d'you mean?' He had one of my hands, stroking it, and he frowned a little. I suppose he thought I'd lost my memory. 'Still feeling muddled, my love?'

'No. "*Me*",' I repeated. '"Love to Dada from Me". You know. In the book.'

His face cleared then. He had an oddly shy look about him too. 'It's my daughter, Genevieve. Rather a long name for a little girl to write.'

'How old?'

'She's eight now. She wasn't six, then, when she wrote that.'

I thought about that for a little while, and then I asked: 'Where is she, Simon?'

'At school. She's at a rather nice little boarding school at Henley-in-Arden. In the holidays she stays with my sister. I see her as often as I can, but—'

'Sundays?'

He nodded. 'That's the usual drill. Not every Sunday. Sometimes I can't make it . . .' I suppose we were both thinking about the Sunday he'd come in to see Caldecott. 'Sometimes she goes to my sister's instead . . . They're very kind, Helen and Bruce. They take her out. They've no children of their own—I think they'd like to adopt her, but I can't make that kind of decision. Not yet.' His fingers tightened round my hand. 'And not alone.' He kept that hand where it was and fumbled clumsily with the other in an inside pocket. 'That's Genevieve.'

I took the colour-snap and looked at it for a long time. She was a pretty little thing, very fair, like the policewoman; and taken from above, smiling up at the camera. She wasn't like Simon at all, and I felt vaguely disappointed. 'She's not like you.'

'No. She's like my wife. Jean.'

'It's an odd camera angle.'

'Think so?' He took the little card from me and looked at it himself. 'That's the angle from which I usually see her, you see. That's why I took it that way.'

I could understand that. 'She's your only child?'

'Now, yes.' His whole face blanked out, all the expression lines erased. 'We had a son. John. He would have been six now. He was—' Simon got up and walked over to the window and stood there with his back to me. 'He was killed with his mother.'

I thought of the broken child in the ambulance again, and grieved for his sake. 'A road accident?'

'Yes.' He said it harshly. 'A road accident.'

'I'm *so* sorry.' What else could I say?

'People always are . . . afterwards. I dare say she

would have been, if she'd lived.' He swung round. 'It was her own fault, Abby. The other driver was exonerated. It was sheer bad driving. That's the awful waste. She was—'

'Don't talk about it,' I said. I was shaken by the change in him. 'I'm sorry I brought it all up.'

He stood there getting a grip on himself for a moment or two. Then he relaxed and came back to the bed. 'Well, perhaps you see now why I'm so keen on road safety and good driving. It became an obsession for a little while, after that.'

'Yes, Simon, I understand.'

'No, you don't. Not altogether . . . If she hadn't died I think I'd have wanted to kill her. She killed my son, Abby.'

'You're very bitter still?'

He nodded. 'I'm afraid I am. It's my Achilles' heel. You must forgive me.' He tried to smile then. 'How silly—I came only to cheer you up, and all I've done is to disturb you. Forgive me.'

'There's nothing to forgive,' I told him. 'I was clumsy . . . Thank you for lending me the books, Simon. I will try, truly. While you're here, would you get them out of that bag for me? I can get some practice in while I'm here.'

'I don't think you ought to do anything but rest.' But he got out the books for me, just the same, and foraged in the bottom of the bag for my pen and notebook, and gave me my compact as well. 'I suppose you'll be wanting this?'

'I haven't dared to look at myself yet,' I confessed. 'Do I look a mess?'

'No, you couldn't . . . Just a bit bruised. There's nothing that'll scar. I think your gums probably got the worst of it. You must have been daydreaming with your mouth open! Go easy with the lipstick for a day or two.'

'I wish Miss Meadows would let me get up.' I flipped open the compact and looked. He was right. I had only a swollen lip and a red mark on my cheek to show for it. 'There's no need for me to be slacking here like this.'

'Well, I hope she won't. Not today . . . Abby, will you come out with me when you're free?' He smiled, and all the strained lines went. 'Not just to deliver watches, but properly.'

I sighed. 'I told you—'

'Please.' He sounded very serious. 'Please, Abby. You see . . . I'd like you to meet Genevieve. I'd like to drive you over to Henley to see her. You'll get on like a house on fire. She must get bored, going out with me by herself. She needs feminine company too, someone other than teachers.'

'There's your sister.'

'Helen? That's different. You know how it is— Helen's her auntie, and she's older than I am. She's part of the set-up. But you—you'd be a breath of fresh air for her.'

The way he was looking at me I had no choice. 'All right,' I agreed. 'I'd like to very much.'

'Good enough.' He smiled properly then. 'We'll fix it.'

*

When Miss Meadows came, after tea, Tom came too. She checked the back of my head, took my pulse rapidly, and said: 'All right, Nurse. You can get dressed tomorrow and see how you feel. And don't play the fool. Go back to bed if you're shaky.' She tossed her black over-permed head at Tom— she had a good many silly gestures like that—and said in a snide sort of way: 'I don't suppose you want me to play gooseberry?' and flounced out, with a good deal of hip-work.

'How arch can they get?' Tom murmured. Then he sat on the edge of the bed and held both my hands. 'Abby, I've been an idiot. I've treated you abominably lately. I suppose I've been so damned busy that I didn't realise I was neglecting you until B. J. Williams told me.'

'*B.J.* told you?'

'Tore strips off me . . . I ran into her in town yesterday and took her for a coffee because she suggested it, and then all I got was a mark one lecture. Can that girl talk! I felt about one inch high when she'd finished with me, I can tell you.'

It ought to have been a relief, but strangely it wasn't. 'So that's what you were doing in the—'

'You heard, of course. I might have known the grapevine would get on to it. You can't blow your nose in this place without everyone making a drama of it. Still, your little adventure seems to have stolen the limelight now. Heroine of the hour and all that.'

'Heroine?' I laughed, and it hurt my lip. 'Fat lot of heroics *I* indulged in. I was a sitting target . . .

Tom, have they found out yet who it was?'

'Not yet. But the Super's having a raid on all the coffee-bars and so forth tonight, he says. They can't identify the old purple hearts and whatnot as coming from here, of course. But it so happens that they took a load of those Barbalac capsules. You remember we had the first batch? And then they changed the colour because they were too like Amytal?'

'Yes. They were—'

'All the other hospitals have the revised ones, with the black stripe—so if they find any plain ones, well, that ties it up with the Royal. We ought to have returned them, I gather, but there seems to have been some failure of communications between the dispenser and the department.' He grinned. 'You know what a vague old thing Mr Partington is.'

'I do,' I said. 'That's clever, isn't it? There *were* a lot there. They didn't seem to use them very often. There were more of those than anything, probably.'

'Twelve boxes, actually. The only thing is . . .' He was frowning now.

'Yes?'

'They seem to think—the police, I mean—that somebody else was involved.'

'How do you mean?'

'Someone inside.'

I stared at him. 'You surely don't mean *me*? Or Joe?'

'I don't know who they mean. But they said

somebody must have tipped these people off about the enormous quantity the place seems to have been carrying compared with other hospital Cas departments, and—'

'It does, I expect. But you know why that is. It's because some of the physicians spin out their clinics so long that the dispensary is closed when they finish, and they've been dispensing things like sleeping tablets themselves and getting Sister to stock them.'

'I know all about them, but it'd take an insider to know it. And somebody must have tipped them off about the time, too. From three to four's about the only time the gate porter leaves his window and gets stuck into a meal in his lodge. The rest of the time he has the ambulance park in full view and he'd see anyone who got in.'

'Well, *I* didn't tip anyone off, I can assure you! And I can't believe that Joe would, either. He's a lazy old devil, but he's too old a hand to fall for that kind of thing.'

Tom began to tread carefully. '*I* know that. Only I gather somebody put a squeal in to Matron about your having been a bit careless with the keys on Three, and they did have some stuff missing recently—oh, only a few amphetamine tablets—so you may find yourself being questioned or something.'

I was furious. 'Tom, who told you this?'

'B.J., actually. She reckoned Sister Knight was thinking it could be your fault. So it looks a bit bad for you, now that this Cas thing's happened.'

'But that's stupid!' I said. 'If I'd been in on it I

wouldn't have been coshed so hard, I hope. I'd just have had a token bruise or two. Besides, my *only* carelessness with the keys on Three was in walking off with them one evening. And that wasn't dangerous . . . As for amphetamines being missing, they were missing when I first went there. Knight told *me* she suspected one of the night people who'd been missing out on sleep. To think I always liked her! How wrong I was.'

Tom made noncommittal noises and traced the bedspread pattern with one finger. 'Oh, well . . .'

'Look,' I blazed, 'whose side are you *on*, for Pete's sake? Hers or mine?'

'Well, yours, obviously. I'm only telling you what I've heard. You'd be mad if I *didn't*.'

That was true enough. 'I'm sorry. Blame my poor head. I'm thoroughly jumpy.'

'Then don't be.' He leaned over and kissed me firmly, right on my bruised mouth. 'Abby, let's go out somewhere when they discharge you. Shall we?'

I pushed him away. 'Oh, Tom! For weeks I made the best of myself, never had a shiny nose, and nobody noticed me. Now that I look like a squashed tomato I get two invitations in one day. It's fantastic.'

'Two?' Tom looked up. 'Oh? Whose was the other?'

'Simon Dell, that's all. Your hero.' I could have kicked myself as soon as it was said.

'*Dell* asked you out?' He got off the bed and stood up straight. 'I see. Well, that's that, then.'

'Oh, don't be silly, Tom. I expect he was sorry for me.'

'Did you say you'd go?'

I had to lie about that, because it was too complicated to explain without going into the question of Genevieve. 'I more or less left it in the air, actually.'

'But I thought you didn't like him.'

'I didn't like your devotedness to him. I suppose I'm jealous. And I was annoyed when you got hurt in his boat.' I waited, but he didn't say anything, so I added: 'Well, changing your half day and everything . . . It hurt me at the time.'

'Oh, Abby!' He kissed me again. I wasn't really in a position to stop him, and he did it several times. I think his lips must have been on my eyelids when Simon walked in, because when I opened them again he was just leaving. He closed the door with a decisive little snap.

Tom said: 'Who was that?'—and laughed when I told him.

I didn't see either of them next day, and although Sister Cracken let me get up in a dressing gown while she waited for Home Sister to bring me some mufti over she kept me mewed up in the side-ward just the same as before. 'Matron says you're not to hurry yourself,' she told me comfortably. 'And I should think not, after that experience. My goodness, the hooligans there are about! Though mind you, one of the reasons they put a night porter down there full time in the first place was so that there wouldn't be that kind of trouble. So what that Joe was doing to let it happen I can't think. Sleeping, I suppose.'

'Maybe,' I said. 'He seems to keep out of the way most of the time, but he always appears when there's anything to do.'

'It's not going enough. Never mind, you won't have to go back there.'

'No?' I was surprised. 'But I've only just been moved.'

'I dare say. But you're going to theatre, Matron says. Your friend Nurse Leonard is moving to Casualty. She said I could tell you. Oh, and she said something about its being a good idea for you to go there before you take the surgery paper again, and she hoped you'd do better in the State for it . . . Goodness, that's only three weeks away, isn't it? How time does fly!'

'I know,' I said. 'Don't remind me, Sister. I ought to be swotting.'

'Not today, you won't, young woman. You just read something light, and relax.' She gathered up my used crocks and beamed at me. 'Now, I must go and see my ladies.' The patients were always 'ladies' to Sister Cracken.

When she had gone I fished out *Sweet Roman Hand* again and got on with my practice in the back of my Dietetics notebook, and tried not to think about Simon's back going out of the door. One of the first things I would do when I got out again, I planned, would be to go and get that broadnibbed pen . . . I wrote twenty alphabets straight off, and the last one was certainly a good deal more shapely than the first. Quicker, too. I was getting into the rhythm of if now.

I began to think about the move to theatre, which was more than I could have hoped for. Something had certainly softened Matron up. I suppose she was really trying to make up to me for the thumping I'd had—which didn't sound as though she suspected me of tipping off the thieves. I thought about the team I'd be working with, and extended my practice with a pageful of *Sister Pleydell is married. Staff Beddoes is a flirt. Con Riley is too friendly with Fletcher.* After a while I tore out a double page from the middle of the book and began carefully: *Dear Simon . . .*

I didn't get any farther. Home Sister arrived with some clothes from my room. 'I thought a jumper and skirt might do, dear,' she said, after she'd told me how sorry she was. 'You won't want that uniform, I'm sure. I expect it's bloodstained, isn't it? I'll put it to the laundry for you, before the stains set. You know how difficult blood is.'

I said I hadn't even seen it. 'I expect it's in the wardrobe, Miss Appleby. Let me get it—they've kept me sitting here so long that I shall turn into a statue if I don't move about.' It wasn't in the wardrobe—one of the refinements of an amenity ward—so I knelt to search the locker cupboard. That made my head thump. I dragged out my dress and apron, and my cuffs. The collar was still pinned to the dress. 'They're here,' I said. There was something else there, too, that I hadn't expected to find. A large masculine handkerchief, heavily bloodstained.

I looked at it again when she had gone, searching for an initial or a laundry mark. It had to be in the last corner I scrutinised. That is life. It was an embroidered 'D'. It had to be Simon's. I had no idea how I had come by it, or when, except that it must have been after Dr Hai arrived in Casualty, and before I found myself in bed.

When Clissold, the senior night nurse, came on at half past eight I tried to find out. 'I don't remember a thing about coming in,' I remarked. 'What happened, exactly?'

'Oh, lots of drama,' she told me. 'No phone call, no message, nothing. There was I, just having a peaceful cuppa, and in charged the Most High with you bleeding like a pig all over his gents' natty suiting, and little Hai trotting along behind. I thought you must be dying, at least, the sweat they were in. So I slung you into bed in something of a hurry.'

'The Most High?'

'Dell, dearie. And what in the name of patience *he* was doing prowling round Cas at that hour I can't conceive. Of course, he *had* been in theatre, earlier, but all the same . . .'

'Very odd,' I said. 'Perhaps he somehow heard the call for Hai, and—'

'And came down out of sheer nosiness? Yes, it'd be like him. He seems to spend a lot more time here than most of them do, that's for sure. Though I don't know how he'd hear the call for Dr Hai. Old

Hai spends all his spare time in his own room playing kinky records, from what I hear . . . Anyhow, there he was, large as life and twice as impatient. Had me running round, I can tell you, to get you into bed. And neither of them had notified Night Sister, if you please! She nearly had a set of jugs when she came up and found you spark out here!'

'I'll bet,' I said. 'And then what happened?'

'Oh, she blew them both out backwards, of course. Hai was scared rigid, but His Nibs just looked through her. Very high and mighty, isn't he?'

'He can be,' I said. 'He must have been pretty peeved if I'd bled all over him.'

'Not to worry,' she told me. 'Bring your drink later—OK?'

I said that suited me. After that I knew what to say in my note. I was very careful with the handwriting—it didn't look like mine at all. I could put it in his pigeonhole as soon as they discharged me: I had no intention of asking Clissold to take it down. Especially after she brought my Ovaltine in and said: 'Come to think of it, it *was* a bit odd, Lord Tomnoddy being down in Cas. I just had the craziest thought, Lake—you don't think *he* clobbered you, do you? To make it look like an outside job?'

I told her not to be so idiotic. 'I should think he can get all the drugs he wants—if he wants them—without resorting to that kind of thing.'

'Yes, but look—if he'd just used his key and

taken the stuff, it'd mean that whoever was on duty would take the can back. But if he made it look like—'

'You're crazy,' I told her. 'He can write scrips for all the drugs he wants to. And why should he want to? He's a pretty healthy specimen himself, and he doesn't need the money.'

'I dare say they *can* all write scrips, but people who are bent enough to want drugs are bent enough to want to get them the hard way, aren't they? Look at that anaesthetist at some hospital in Birmingham who was hooked on ether. And there's Burrows swearing that the new gynae registrar's got dilated pupils and funny moodswings. It makes you wonder.'

'What rot you talk,' I said. 'Night-duty gossip gets sillier all the time.'

She smiled. 'It always did! Now, anything else you'd like? Food, drink, anything?'

'Nothing, thanks,' I told her.

'Just peace and quiet, I suppose?'

'Something like that.'

I lay there for a long time after I'd put the light out, wondering why Simon had come down to the department, what B.J. had been saying to Tom, and what I ought to do about it all. I don't think I came to any useful conclusion.

CHAPTER EIGHT

I DIDN'T see Simon, and I didn't see Tom, and I had no reply to my note and hadn't the heart to send another. But I kept on practising my handwriting. They let me go on Friday, and on Saturday I took the surgery paper again. Miss Black said: 'As you're the only re-taker we may as well get it over before you go back on duty, I think. I've got round the consultants and the SSO to set a paper just for you, so let's hope you sail through it this time. You *can*, you know.'

'I'll try,' I said.

'I'll stay with you myself, while I get the junior papers marked. And I'll have my fingers crossed for you,' she said, and we sat alone in the schoolroom and I settled down to it.

It was no stiffer than the first paper, but it took me a good deal longer to get through it. I'd bought the broad-nibbed pen, and I was determined that every word should be legible this time. I still remembered everything Simon had said about the last paper, and it still stung.

I was just finishing the final question, one on congenital hip dislocation—I'd really gone to town about that—when Miss Black said: 'Another five minutes, Nurse. Nearly done?'

'Just on the last line,' I told her.

'Well, that gives you two or three minutes to revise, if you need to.' In other words, I'd better read it through carefully while I still had the chance.

When she came over at last to collect the sheaf of papers she stared at them, and then at me. 'Well! My best cap, Nurse Lake, your writing *has* changed! *Very* much clearer. You must have been practising. Yes?'

'Yes,' I admitted. 'Mr—I was told it probably failed me last time. And—well, I suppose it's true enough that it could be dangerous if it was a case of copying medications and someone misread it. So I thought I'd better try.'

She nodded. 'Very true, Nurse . . . Oh, and talking of medications—they've found the person who took those drugs from Casualty, I hear. They were quite right—it *was* an inside job, in a manner of speaking.'

'It was?' I looked up quickly. 'Who, Miss Black?'

'I don't know that I'm supposed to say.' She pushed the papers into their envelope and licked the flap thoughtfully. 'Still, I suppose it'll be common knowledge by the time you get to breakfast tomorrow . . . You know Nurse Reid?'

That really shook me. 'Of course, yes.'

'Seems she has rather an unsavoury boy-friend. Used to go in and visit her when she was on nights down there. That's why Matron had her moved from there, and sent you down instead.'

'But I thought—' I tried to remember exactly what Sister Knight had said at the time. She had certainly given me the impression that Matron was moving me to punish me for 'making an exhibition of myself' by crying on Tom. 'But *I* was the one who was moved, I thought. Reid just came up to replace me, surely.'

Miss Black's eyebrows went up. 'Whatever gave you that idea, Nurse?' She looked at her fob-watch, and sat down frankly for five minutes' gossip. 'Look, Nurse Reid had this friend, as I said, and I imagine he was merely cultivating her because she was the Casualty nurse. Certainly he first met her through coming in after some brawl or other— you'd think that would be enough to warn her, wouldn't you? . . . At any rate, it appears he's what's called a 'pusher', if that means anything to you?'

'Well, it's a man who distributes drugs, I suppose.'

'*And* gives them away, to create new addicts, Nurse. It seems this man was picked up with a pocketful of those Barbalac capsules, and for some reason they're sure they came from here.'

I explained about the stripe on all the batches except ours. 'But how did Reid come into it?'

'Because he tried to blame her—she was horrified, of course—and the end of it is that he comes up to court quite soon. I don't know if they'll need you. Just catching him in unauthorised possession was good enough for them to arrest him, it seems, and they've opposed bail, so there you are. I suppose that through calling in to see Nurse Reid he got the hang of where things were kept and so on, and what time things happened, and then it was child's play.'

'Do you suppose that he expected her to be there—and that if she had been she'd have been knocked out the same as I was?' I said.

'I wouldn't put it past him.'

'She'll feel awful. She'll feel she's been made a fool of, won't she?'

Miss Black smiled. 'Oh, she'll get over it. Next time perhaps she'll be a little more selective. She's quite a sensible girl, really. I'd say this was a bit of a lapse on her part . . . He had a legitimate excuse for being here that night, too, that's the odd thing. His brother's a patient, and he's been pretty ill, so they let him visit extra late, and I suppose the opportunity was too good to miss . . . A man who came in after a car crash. Jeffrey somebody. Maybe you admitted him?'

'"Call-me-Jeff",' I said. 'He's a driving instructor. So that's his brother? I had one lesson with him, nearly crashed into Mr—into another car, and gave up the idea. He wasn't much of an instructor. Not much of a driver, either, or he wouldn't have had six people in a Mini that night.' I still remembered that night. 'Or so Mr Dell said at the time.'

'Mr Dell? Yes, that's another thing. *He's* got his problems too, I hear, poor man. He's been sent for this morning to go to his daughter. She's at a boarding school somewhere, I think.'

I nodded. 'Henley-in-Arden.'

'Is that where it is? Well, they seem to be worried about her . . . It's certainly odd how head injuries follow that man around. What with Mr Fitzgibbon, and—well, yours had nothing to do with him, of course. The little girl had a bad fall in the gym, apparently. Climbing ropes without supervision when she wasn't supposed to, or something. I suppose he'll be bringing her back if she's fit to be moved. He told the theatre to be ready, in case . . . Goodness, theatre—aren't you on at two o'clock?'

'Yes,' I said. I felt cold. 'I am.'

'Then fly to your lunch, child, quickly. I'd forgotten all about it. And don't worry about this paper— I'm sure you'll pass this time, if it's only for neatness!'

Sister Pleydell was laying up her trolley when I arrived and Staff Beddoes was charging in and out of the annexe looking hot and bothered for once. Beddoes said: 'Well, thank God you're here, so that I can scrub. I'll have to do swabs and things, because Sister's assisting, and Leonard's gone to nights.'

I took the glove-drum she was carrying. 'OK. You go ahead and scrub. What's coming up?'

'A decompression. It's Mr Dell's daughter, so let's not have any slip-ups, Lake.'

'He's not doing it himself, surely?'

'No, of course not. Mr Harriman's operating. But he's sure to hang around. You may have to scoop him up off the floor if anything goes wrong. You know what doting dads are.'

I couldn't see it the way she did. I wished I could. 'I wish he'd keep away,' I said. 'He *oughtn't* to watch. It creates tension, as well as being bad for him.'

'Try telling him that!' Beddoes scrubbed away at her hands under the mixer tap. 'Frankly, he's not my favourite person to argue with. Gown me up, will you? Six-and-a-half gloves. Then you'll be ready for Pa Harriman.'

When I had tied her tapes I walked over to look through the porthole in the anaesthetic-room door. Dr Hai was sitting there waiting, that was all. And then Sister Pleydell wriggled her eyebrows over her mask and sent me to ask the tech to get another oxygen cylinder up from stores. By the time I'd run him to earth, out on the corridor balcony snatching a quick smoke, and got back again they were there. A little silver-haired girl lying very still on the trolley, with a bluish-purple dusky skin and slow snoring breathing, and Simon, white-faced, holding both her hands and looking quite out of place in a blue fisherman's jersey.

I reached down an unsterile gown from the top of the cupboard and touched his arm gently. 'You going in with her?'

He went on watching little Dr Hai filling his syringe, and then looked at me blankly. 'What was that?'

'You'll need a gown,' I reminded him.

'Oh, yes . . . You're here now?'

'Yes,' I said. I took his hands away from his daughter's and got him to slip his arms into the gown. 'I'm so sorry.'

He took Genevieve's hands again. 'I must be bad

medicine. Things always happen to the people I care about . . . Isn't Harriman ready yet?'

I glanced through the porthole. 'He and the SSO are just scrubbing. I'll have to go and dress them now.'

'The SSO? But it's his weekend off.'

'I know,' I said. 'I thought Sister was to assist. He must have come in specially.'

'Harriman's a good man.'

'Yes,' I said distinctly. 'He's *excellent*. Don't fuss.'

'I'm coming in. I've got to.'

'All right,' I said. 'All right, Simon. But relax.'

When I was tying Mr Harriman's mask he said: 'Her father out there, Nurse?'

I said he was.

'He coming in?'

'I think so, sir.'

'You couldn't dissuade him?'

'I didn't try, sir,' I said. 'He's made up his mind.'

He grunted something, and he and the SSO exchanged looks, and then he said: 'All right. Let's have her in, then.'

It went on for a long time. Simon stood beside me against the spare bit of wall and didn't move. I left him three times: once to fish a small burr out of the steriliser, once to top up the lotion bowls, and once to change Sister's mask when a fine arterial spurt painted a scarlet line across it. I wished I could do something to prevent him from listening to the vibration of the trephine on that little skull, and the scrape of the Gigli's saw, but there was nothing I could possibly do. Everyone in the theatre was very quiet. There was none of the usual irrelevant chit-chat between Mr Harriman and the SSO. If Simon hadn't been there I knew they would have been letting down the tension by discussing golf, or the theatre, or maybe the latest idiocy perpetrated by the management committee. As it was there was just the creak of the SSO's rubber boots as he transferred his weight from one leg to the other, and the faint hiss of the anaesthetic machine, and the uncertain rhythm of Genevieve's respiration, punctuated by the occasional click of an artery forceps against the stainless steel receiver.

Dr Hai was beginning to look anxious towards the end. Mr Harriman was aware of it at once, and looked up to say: 'All right, Hai, you can let her up. I've nearly done.' Then he flicked his first glance at Simon. 'Not to worry, old man. She'll do. I've removed a sizeable clot, but there's no more bleeding.'

Sister wagged her head at me a moment later to go and get the kettle on. I had the tea-tray in the surgeons' room three minutes later. Dr Hai went scuttling off somewhere; the SSO put his head in to say: 'Sorry, can't stop. They want me downstairs'; Mr Harriman went straight through into the changing room, and Simon walked in slowly and pitched his length on the floor.

Mr Harriman, in a bizarre pink singlet and briefs, heard the bump and darted out to help me to turn Simon over. 'Poor devil,' he said. 'He shouldn't have watched.'

'I know, sir,' I agreed. 'But he had to. You'd have done just the same.'

I went to fetch brandy, and poured a good measure of it, from Sister's emergency bottle, into a medicine glass. When I got back Simon was sitting up, leaning against the armchair. He drank the brandy obediently, then flushed suddenly and pushed me away. 'Thanks,' he said. He might as well have been saying it to a bus-conductress. He stood up after a minute or so, and drank some of the tea I'd poured for him, and Mr Harriman came back knotting his tie, and I left them to it.

It was just that he was worried about Genevieve, I told myself. But I thought of the last time I had seen him, just the back of his head as he walked out of the sideward, and that didn't help at all. I thought about him all the time we were clearing up the theatre, and Staff Beddoes must have picked up some of it by telepathy, because she said: 'He's got guts, I'll say that for him.' She clashed a bunch of Spencer-Wells on the steriliser tray on the draining board. 'Damned if *I* could have stood there and watched it. He OK now?'

I shrugged. 'Think so. He flopped in the surgeons' room. I gave him some brandy out of the cupboard.'

'How are the mighty fallen! So he does have a weak spot, after all.'

'Several, I should think,' I said. 'He's not a fish . . . Some of these elevators belong in the other theatre—shall I take them back?'

'Not likely. They've got no end of our stuff. One day before Matron's inventory we shall have to have a sort-out . . . I didn't know he was married, to tell the truth. Wonder what she's like? Some glam blonde with a rich daddy, I suppose. That's the usual form.'

I didn't see any reason to tell her that Simon was a widower, so I didn't answer that one. I dumped my tray of stuff into the big steriliser, and then got out the squeegee and began on the floor.

Somehow I was never on duty when Simon had a list that week, but I did see Genevieve. I went up three times to the children's private wing when Sister was off. Staff Hunton was a good sort, and she only said: 'Well, I suppose you theatre people have a special interest in her.' The first time she was asleep, two turns of bandage and a fluff of hair showing above the sheet. The second time she sat up and talked to me. She was an attractive and intelligent little thing, but small for her age. 'What's your name?' she wanted to know.

'Nurse Lake,' I told her.

'I mean your first name. Mine's Genevieve. Sister calls me Jenny—isn't that silly? What's your *first* name?'

'Abby,' I said. 'It's short for Annabel.'

'That's a funny name, Abby. I think I've heard Annabel before, though. Yes, I have. I heard Daddy say it once to Auntie Helen. I remember, because I thought he said "Animal" at first. He knows somebody called Annabel.'

'Oh?' I wished I flushed less easily. 'And what did he say about her?'

She corrugated her forehead and pursed up her pink bud of a mouth. 'I think he said he'd lent her a book. Yes, Auntie Helen was looking for this book, and he said: "I lent it to Annabel." That's right. I expect she's his sweetheart. Auntie Helen said it was time he found one, because he's very— very edible.'

'Edible?' I laughed. 'I think you mean eligible.'

'Do I? What does it mean?'

'Oh . . . It means he's a nice man. The sort of man that ladies like, I suppose.'

'They don't, you know.' Her gilt-tipped lashes starred out round her blue eyes. 'Mrs Grocock *hates* him. She thinks he's a very untidy man.'

'Who's Mrs Grocock, Genevieve?'

'Oh, she looks after him when I'm at school. She's a very funny lady. Ever so fat, and she keeps her hat on all the time in the house. She's sort of squashy all over, and she keeps saying that her feet hurt. And she's always putting things where Daddy can't find them, and he gets *so* cross. She came instead of Mummy, you see.'

'I see,' I said. I wanted to howl. 'I have to go now. Shall I come again?'

'Oh, yes, *please*. I'll draw a picture of you and give it to you when you come, if you like. I'm quite good at doing people, only I can't always get their legs the right shape. Legs are hard, aren't they?'

'Very hard,' I agreed. 'I can never get them right,

either. But horses' legs are the worst—the back ones.'

She beamed. 'You're just like me, aren't you? Oh, do come and see me again . . . if you can spare the time,' she added politely. 'I expect you get rather busy.'

'Not too busy for that,' I assured her.

The third time I went up her cubicle was empty. Staff Hunton said: 'You're just ten minutes too late, Lake. He's taken her off for a holiday somewhere. Near Cannes, I think he said. Nice to be some people, isn't it? I'd be glad to get as far as Brighton, myself.'

'Me too,' I said. And then I went back to the theatre and switched on the sterilisers, and filled the lotion bowls, and sorted drums, and laid up trolleys, and did all the other little jobs that made up my day. And instead of watching Simon's hands I watched Tom's. He still had strapping on one cheek, and that reminded me of Simon too.

At the end of the list he came into the scrub-room to be untied and asked: 'Well? What are you doing this afternoon? I see it's your half day.'

'Is it?' I said. 'I haven't even looked at the list.'

'No, but I have. And it's mine too. So—?'

'All right,' I told him obligingly, 'I suppose I did half promise.'

'Where shall we go?'

I said the first thing that came into my head. 'Flicks?'

'Oh, very romantic!'

I pulled his gown off. 'I didn't know it was meant to be romantic. If that's what you're looking for perhaps you'd better take someone else. Clissold, for example. Or Staff Beddoes. Or why not B.J.? Yes, take B.J. I daresay she's the romantic sort, deep down inside.'

'Don't be like that, Abby.' Tom tugged off his cap and dropped it into the bin. 'I'm serious. We've got a lot of lost time to make up. Besides, I've something to tell you, specially. Suppose you slack this afternoon, and have a bath and do your hair and all that nonsense. Then I'll pick you up at six and we'll go and eat somewhere lush. Yes?'

'Well, yes,' I said, without enthusiasm. 'If that's what you want to do.'

He knocked on the taps too violently, and water shot over his white theatre slacks. 'Damn!' he said. 'For heaven's sake show *some* interest. Shall I come at six or not? Do you want me to?'

There wasn't much choice, without hurting him. 'Yes, please,' I said, as politely as Genevieve. 'Thank you, Tom.'

The place he had heard about in the common room wasn't as lush as he'd been told. It was one of those bogus old-world places full of reproduction oak and mass-produced horse brasses, with Musak drifting in from a hidden speaker. But the rollmops and the steak Diane were perfect, and Tom said the Stilton was exactly at the critical point, whatever that meant. When we had our coffee I said: 'Well?

We've done nothing but sit and guzzle so far—and very nice too—but didn't you say you had something to tell me?'

'I have.' He put more sugar into his cup and stirred it, smiling to himself. 'Abby, I've put in for a consultancy in South Africa.'

I was completely taken aback. 'South Africa! But you—'

'I know. I said I'd go to the States, and then I said I'd stay here . . . But it's an opportunity I can't let pass. And I think I'll probably get it, too. They're short of applicants.'

'Good luck, then,' I said flatly. I knew I ought to be saying a good deal more, but there didn't seem to be anything to say. 'Good luck, Tom.'

'Thanks for your enthusiasm! . . . Well, what I'm trying to say is—Abby, if I get it, will you come with me?'

Six months earlier I'd probably have jumped at the chance. Now I simply sat there, bewildered and uncertain. He'd practically proposed to me—and wasn't that what I'd always banked on? After a while I said: 'Go with you, Tom?'

He smiled quickly and reached out to put his hand over mine. 'Lovey, I'm asking you to marry me. I thought it was what we'd both—well, taken for granted all along. Isn't it?'

'Oh, Tom,' I said feebly, 'I just—Now that you've asked me I simply don't know what to say. Honestly. I don't *know* what to say.'

'I see.' He took his hand away then and poured himself another cup of coffee with elaborate care.

Black. And he never took it black. 'You want to think it over?'

'But it's no use doing even that, is it, until you're sure of the job?' That was sheer evasion, and I knew it. 'After all, you can't be sure, Tom.'

He had stopped smiling. 'Seems I can't be sure of anything else, either. I always thought—'

'So did I,' I said miserably. 'Only now it's different.'

He looked at me hard. 'Someone else?'

'Not really, no. It's just *me*. I don't know what I want, that's the trouble.'

'All right. Think it over, Abby. Then tell me. Hm?'

'I'll do that,' I promised. 'Why are you so sure you have a good chance?'

'Not many applicants, I told you. And Dell and one or two others are recommending me. Seems Dell has some pull.'

'Tom, was it his idea? In the first place?' It seemed to me that it was a very important point.

'No, of course not. It was advertised, and everyone in the common room saw it. Matter of fact, it was *la* Meadows who thought it was my kind of thing. Why?'

'I just wondered.'

'The money's fabulous. Far better than I could ever hope to get here. It's a three-year arrangement in the first place, with the option to renew. Of course it works rather differently out there. You're paid by . . .'

I wasn't really listening. I was thinking of all the

things I'd said to Triss about Tom in the past. The times I'd cried. The awful let-down it had been when he changed his half day. The way I'd been jealous of his hero-worship of Simon. It all seemed a long time ago.

I was still abstracted when he dropped me back at the Home and kissed me goodnight. 'Little Dolly Daydream,' he said. 'What are you pondering?'

I couldn't tell him. 'Wondering whether I've passed that wretched surgery paper this time,' I said. 'And how I'll do in the State. Less than three weeks to go.'

'But what does it matter? If you're getting married it isn't going to matter two hoots whether you're State Registered or not, lovey. Is it?'

'It matters to *me*,' I said obstinately. 'I'm not going to do three years hard labour and then not qualify at the end of it. Not if I have to take it all three times.'

'All three times?'

'We're only allowed three goes.'

'Darling, you'll barely have time for one! If I take this job I'll have to go inside a month.'

That wasn't really relevant, but I hadn't the heart to tell him so. 'We'll see,' I said. 'Goodnight, Tom. It was a jolly good meal. I enjoyed it.'

'And you're not going to keep me waiting for an answer, are you?'

'No,' I promised, 'I won't keep you waiting. But I have to have time to think. You've taken me by surprise, Tom. I don't want to make a mistake.'

'Try to tell me by Monday. They're interviewing in London next week.'

'Whatever I say won't make any difference to that, will it?'

He looked uncomfortable. 'It will actually. If I'm married, or about to be, it'll help. They're not keen on a bachelor, I gather. They want what's called a "family man". One who'll settle, you know.'

I understood a good many things then. Triss had always said that Tom's career came before his marrying instinct, and that most registrars married to forward their career interests. 'I see,' I said. 'It's like that.'

'Yes, it's—Oh, hell, Abby! Not it *isn't* like that. You've got it all wrong.'

'But if you don't get the job, you don't want to get married just yet.'

'Well, on registrar's pay it can be a bit dicey. We've always agreed on that, haven't we? I mean, we talked about it once before, and we came to the conclusion that it would be tough going.'

I didn't remind him that he was the one who had come to that conclusion. As far as I was aware I had never expressed an opinion. 'I expect you're right, Tom. I've no head for figures . . . Look, I *must* go. Miss Appleby'll be chasing me up if I'm late in.'

'Yes, I suppose she will . . . Goodnight, Abby. And let me know.'

I hadn't seen very much of Triss for a week or two, but I ran into her in the utility room, filling her bottle. She said: 'Hi! Recovered? You look positively dazed. What's up?'

'I'm a bit stunned,' I said. 'What do you know? Tom's asked me to marry him.'

She dropped the bottle in the sink and hugged me. 'Well, congratulations! You were beginning to despair, weren't you? When's it to be? Has he bought you a ring yet?'

It was then, with Triss taking it for granted, that I knew I couldn't go through with it. 'I didn't say I'd accepted,' I reminded her. 'I only said he'd asked me.'

'But this is what you've been waiting for!'

'I know,' I said. 'And now it's a bit of an anti-climax. I suppose you think I'm crazy.'

'I don't know what to think, frankly.' Triss's face was screwed up with bewilderment. 'Oh, Abby, it isn't—well, it *isn't* Simon Dell, is it?'

'You must be joking,' I told her. 'Do hurry up with that kettle. I want to make some tea. It's odd, whenever I drink coffee I always want tea afterwards to quench my thirst . . . We went to that new place—what's it called? The Manor Farm?—that the men have discovered. It's not bad—rather a phoney set-up, but the food was wonderful.'

Triss didn't say anything. She just looked at me, and then got on with her bottle-filling. But her face said a good deal.

I went through Reid's pamphlets about the QAs when I was in bed. It sounded a good life. Better than Tutorial, at any rate. There was no harm, I decided, in filling up the form asking for more information. It would mean travel, and surely it would mean meeting plenty of decent men? Tom and Simon weren't the only men on earth. I remembered what I'd said to Simon about being the last man on earth. That, too, seemed a very long time ago.

CHAPTER NINE

ON Sunday, when I was on theatre call until midnight, Tom rang through to say he wanted to do a myringotomy on a woman from Ward 2. 'No use leaving it,' he said. 'The drum's bulging like crazy, and she's in acute pain. I shan't want anyone but you.'

Miss Meadows came up to anaesthetise. She'd been fetched from her bed, and she wasn't exactly pleased. 'They never used to bother with general anaesthetics for these things,' she grumbled. 'I can't think why they do now.'

'Can't you?' Tom said from the scrub sink. 'You might if you'd ever had an acute otitis yourself. People used not to get a shot for tooth drilling, either. I suppose you think that's coddling, too?'

'I do, frankly. People are getting soft.' She looked across at me. 'Don't you think so, Nurse Lake?'

I tried to compromise. 'Maybe people aren't as tough as they used to be . . . but if so, that's all the more reason for using painkillers. I don't see much virtue in suffering just to mortify the flesh, or whatever they call it . . . Do I get the patient in now? Because the sooner she's done, the sooner you can go back to bed.'

She didn't speak to me after that. I got the

patient on the table and fixed Tom's head-light, and gave him the myringotomy knife and the aural forceps and fished packing out of the drum, and it was all done in five minutes. Miss Meadows stamped off to bed and the ward nurse took the patient down. Tom stayed right where he was, leaning on his forearms on the table.

He watched me boil up the things he'd used and put them away, and then he said: 'Well, Abby?'

'Well?' I said.

'Twelve o'clock. Zero hour.'

'Yes.' I looked up at the wall clock with its long red seconds hand jerking round. 'I've been on since eight this morning. Time I got off duty.'

'I don't mean that,' Tom said heavily. 'I meant—well, about us. You said you'd let me know by Monday, and it's Monday morning now.'

Because I hadn't expected to see him that night I had no kind speech prepared, but there was no point in prolonging the thing. It had to be said, once and for all. 'I'm sorry,' I told him. 'I just can't say "yes" unconditionally, Tom, so I'd better say "no". I *am* sorry, believe me. If you'd asked me a few months ago . . . But things have changed. *I've* changed. I suppose I'm older, or something. And part of it's died on me now. I just don't love you enough to drop my job and go haring off to Africa . . . Tom, it isn't that I'm not fond of you. I am. Only it's a big step and I don't feel I can take it.'

'I see.' He was playing with the table, pumping it up and letting it slide down again. 'Well, at least I know where I stand.' The odd thing was that he didn't seem hurt at all, only put out, the way he'd be if I'd been a few minutes late for a date. No more than that. 'Thanks for telling me, Abby.'

I tried again to get through to him. 'Tom, I'm sorry if it's going to muck up the job prospects for you.'

'It won't.' He sounded pretty confident. 'I shan't let it. I shall tell them I'm engaged. It isn't a thing they can prove, after all. And engagements can always be broken, can't they?'

I realised then that I had never really known Tom at all. I had seen what I wanted to see, and not the opportunist career man underneath the charm. That was when it really ended. 'Good luck, then,' I said feebly. 'I hope you get it.' And I walked into the duty room and changed out of my theatre slip into uniform. When I went back to put out the theatre lights before I locked up Tom had gone.

One of the nice things about being on late call was that we had the next day off. I spent the morning lazing in bed, and then I dressed in mufti and went over to second lunch. I knew somebody had been talking about me as soon as I sat down, because everyone round me seemed to be embarking on a fresh conversation. Except B. J. Williams, who sat there, opposite me, with a flaming face, and said nothing at all except: 'Hope your head's better, Lake?'

She buttonholed me on the way out. 'Look, I'm off now until five. Could I have a word with you in your room? Or are you going straight out?'

I told her I hadn't any plans at all, really, and added: 'Come over now, if you like.'

'I've got a phone call to make first. I'll be with you in about five minutes,' she said. 'What number are you?'

'Sixty-two, second floor. You know, the corner one with the phone extension that they keep for theatre bods?'

She nodded. 'Yes, of course. I won't be long.'

When she came knocking at my door she still looked uncomfortable. Excited, too, in a way. I said: 'I suppose you've come to confess about that day I saw you with Tom Fitzgibbon. Is that it? Because if so—'

She was surprised. 'Well, partly. You see, Lake, they all take it for granted that *you're* his girl.'

'And you thought it your duty to tell him he was treating me badly?'

'It wasn't like that, no.'

'He *says* you lectured him.'

'You've got it all wrong, Lake. Listen—Tom asked me to marry him, and—'

'He *what*?' I said. 'When was this?'

'That day we were in the Grand, of course.'

I sat down on the bed. 'Just a minute. Let's get this straight. He asked you to marry him when he was—'

'Well, he'd hinted at it when he was warded, you see, only I didn't take him seriously. I thought it was just the concussion, and that you'd had a bit of a squabble, and it was sort of reaction. You know.'

I remembered her face when she had come out of

his side-ward. 'Yes,' I said, 'I know. Well, go on.'

'So then we ran into one another in town—oh, it was quite accidental—and we went for coffee, and he asked me again. Of course I said: "What about Abby Lake?" And *he* said what about you, and that you'd made it pretty plain that there was nothing doing, and all that, and that you weren't really his type at all. Too tense, he said, actually.' She looked up apologetically. 'Anyhow, I said I wouldn't have him until he'd come clean with you about it, and made quite sure that you weren't interested. I said if he didn't ask you straight out, then I would.'

'Yes. I told you, he said you lectured him.'

'I suppose I did. You see I thought you were still keen, and that he was just in a rebound phase, sort of . . . Oh, I'm terribly fond of him, but I couldn't break anything up like that. I told him he had to definitely finish with you before I'd even consider it. And now . . .' She began to falter. 'Now—'

'And now what?'

'Well, now he says it's all off between you and he's asked me again.'

'You've said "yes", of course?'

'More or less . . . Lake, are you *awfully* mad with me?'

'Not in the least,' I said. I smiled at her. 'You'll probably stand the climate a lot better than I should. My skin's too dry already.'

'Climate?' She frowned. 'How do you mean?'

'Hasn't he told you about this South African job?' I added meanly: 'This job where he has to be married or about to be? I thought that was the whole object of the exercise!'

She flushed. 'No, he didn't. He did say there was a consultancy in the offing, but he didn't say where . . . Lake, you don't mean he just wants to get engaged to somebody so as to—Oh, *no*. Not *Tom*?'

'Tom,' I said. 'Well, that's how it looks from here. But don't let me influence you, B.J. Only you're a nice girl, and I wouldn't want to see you hurt.'

'I can't believe it.'

'Then don't. Look, I don't know how his mind works any more. Maybe I never did. That's why I didn't want to marry him. The ball's in your court, old dear. Play it your own way. You'll probably be very happy. He'll go a long way, will Tom. He's clever, and he's ambitious. And he can be very good company when he likes. You'll be all right.'

In a very small voice she said: 'I do think the *world* of him. And even if it's just that he thinks a wife might be useful, I still want to marry him.'

'Then you're engaged to him?'

'I suppose so. I haven't told anyone officially. I thought I ought to talk to you first.'

'Right,' I said. 'Well, you've talked to me—and all I've done is to sow seeds of doubt in your mind, I suppose. I'm sorry. I'm a cat. I do wish you happiness, B.J. I mean that. And I hope Tom gets all the things he wants too . . . Now, if you'll excuse me, I think I'll get a bath.'

She got up from the bed and went to the door at once. There she looked back uncertainly. 'You don't mind my coming? It's better to have it straightforward, isn't it?'

'Much better,' I agreed. 'Thank you for telling me.'

I didn't go to the bathroom straight away. I had a little weep first. Not because I wanted Tom, but because it was the end of something, and because the manner of it had been hurtful. And I didn't see how B.J. could have so little pride.

Later on I went down to the post-box in the front hall to send off my letter to the QAs. There was a bright postcard in my pigeonhole. A Mediterranean seascape with tiny white houses nestling in a wooded cliff. *Dear Nurse Abby*, it said, *I'm having a lovely time. Daddy got a big fish and we went sailing today. Love from Genevieve Dell*. There was no word from Simon.

The theatre routine went on, day after day, list after list; the SSO, Mr Harriman, Tom—who scarcely spoke to me—and the rest. Even Sir Henry made a comeback to do a partial gastrectomy for a private patient who refused to have anyone less. I seemed to be more exhausted and anti-social every time I went off duty. And then one morning, two days before the Final State, I trudged into the scrub-room and found Simon washing with Tom alongside.

In the sick little moment of recognition I heard Tom saying: 'So I'll be off at the end of the month.'

'Good,' Simon said heartily. 'That's absolutely splendid. Congratulations, Tom.' Then he turned to me, smiling widely, his teeth very white in his tanned face, and said briskly: 'Right, towel, please, Nurse.'

I fished out a sterile towel and brought it to him with the Cheadle forceps, and then went back to open up the glove drum. Tom didn't say anything until I had Simon gowned and masked and he had wandered through to the table with his hands clasped in front of his chest, to wait for the patient. Then he turned his back for me to tie his tapes and said over his shoulder: 'I got that job, Abby. I was just telling Dell. Biddy and I are getting married in a fortnight.'

'Biddy? You mean B.J.? I see.'

'Will you come to the wedding?'

I tightened his neck tapes savagely. 'Maybe.'

'We hoped—Hey! Don't strangle me!'

'I'd like to,' I said. He could take that whichever way he liked, I thought. Then I told myself not to be childish. 'It depends on my off-duty, doesn't it?'

It was a long list, and at half-time when we broke off for ten minutes for tea Sister Pleydell said: 'You can take the rest, Nurse Lake. I'm going off now. You've got Mr Riley, and Staff'll be back at lunch-time.'

'I'd love to,' I said. 'They're all fairly routine, I suppose?'

'Yes. Two appendicectomies, an inguinal hernia, and the last's a woman for laparotomy, query new growth.'

'I suppose Mr Fitzgibbon's doing them, is he, Sister?'

'Oh, no, Mr Dell's finishing himself. He knows I've got this dental appointment, and he's quite agreeable to have you instead . . . You're not scared of him, are you?'

'Hardly,' I said. 'Only he's so terribly quick.'

'So are you, Nurse, when you put your mind to it! You'll be all right.'

The appendicectomies went smoothly enough. So did the hernia. Then, when we were towelling up the laparotomy, Con Riley went to answer the phone and came back to say: 'They want Mr Fitzgibbon in Three, urgently. Shall I tell them to get somebody else? Blake's haemorrhaged again, Sister says.'

'Tell 'em to get the SSO,' Tom said.

Simon lifted his head. 'Rubbish. You can clear off, Tom. Nurse can assist me perfectly well. Can't you, Nurse Lake?'

I was trembling. Not because of the job, but because of Simon's nearness, I think. 'I'll try, sir. But I'm not awfully quick, you know.'

'We don't want to hurry this one. We don't know what we may find. Cut along, Tom.' I moved in to take Tom's place, and Con shoved my trolley closer to me, and when Tom had gone Simon said: 'That's your friend the driving instructor. Blake.'

'Oh?' I slapped the scalpel into his hand.

'Brother to your drug-pushing pal.'

'Fine friends I seem to have!' I felt almost gay as I mopped along the thin red line of his incision and reached for artery forceps.

'Indeed.' He went with delicate deliberation

through a muscle layer. 'Clip that fellow, will you?'

I got the bleeding point and mopped again. I had time to glance at the patient's notes hanging on the anaesthetic trolley. 'You think this *is* a neoplasm? She's only twenty-six.'

'I don't know. There's a palpable mass, not pulsating, and it could be anything. Pictures weren't much help.'

I began to worry straight away. I passed him a couple of retractors and kept my hand on the one on my side. 'You mean it could be a tubal gestation? In that case—'

'Could be. It won't be viable, if it is.'

Con Riley knew as well as I did that if it was a tubal we could be in for massive haemorrhage. There might be a lot of fluid pocketed there too. When I looked at him he passed me the big sucker straight away. I watched Simon's fingers and felt cold, trying to remember all the emergency routine, tilting the table, stepping up the drip, packing the wound, and all the rest of it. With my free hand I pulled a pack of the biggest abdominal mops right to the edge of the trolley.

Simon went on exploring, carefully dipping his long fingers under the retracted peritoneum, looking blindly at the wall opposite him and concentrating all his senses into his hands. Then he said: 'Here it is.' He eased part of a glistening capsule through the incision. 'Tubal it is. I'll have a lengthen the incision a bit. Then we'll tie off and resect. Clamps, please, Nurse.'

I don't think any of us really breathed during the next five minutes. It needed such a tiny slip to let go the floodgates. But it was superbly done. I'd known it would be, really. Simon didn't make that kind of mistake.

When we were putting in the tension sutures he nodded at the receiver on the bottom shelf of my trolley. 'Get that to the path. lab., won't you? It's a pretty historic specimen. They'll want to pickle it. They don't often go that far without rupturing.'

I wanted to tell him that it was pretty historic for the operation to be done so safely and neatly too, but I couldn't find the words. Miss Meadows did poke her head forward to say: 'Jolly fine show, sir, I must say!' but she made it sound as though she could have done it ten times as well herself, and she only meant it was a good effort for a mere man.

He didn't stay for tea afterwards, but he said: 'I'm nipping down to look at Blake, and to fetch something from the car, and I'll be back. You'll be here, will you?'

'I'll be here,' I said.

I was singing as I scrubbed the instruments. Con Riley said: 'Well, you are a merry little grig today. Nice change, I must say. You've been a regular zombie this last week or so. The sunshine of the great man's smile, is it?'

'Could be,' I said easily. 'He's very good-tempered today, isn't he?'

'So he should be, after his little bask. Some of us have to work for our livings. Still, that tubal was a cracking job, I'll say that for him. He's got good hands, has our Simon.'

'I'm sure he'd be touched,' I said. 'Is Staff back yet?'

'She's been in, yes, but she's gone to first lunch. She said we could go to second. *If* we were clear in time. I was supposed to go to first, but with Sister off—'

'Go when you want to,' I said. 'I can cope now.'

He gave me an odd look. 'Ever felt you weren't wanted? All right, message received. I'll just dump this lot in the steriliser and then I'll vamoose.'

'And take that specimen to the path. while you're at it,' I said. 'Want me to do the label?'

'I've done it, dearie. I did it while you two were still gloating over the thing . . . Right, I'm off. And don't go doing anything I wouldn't do.'

'I won't,' I said.

It was another quarter of an hour before Simon came up, and I was mopping the floor while I waited for the sand to run out of the big timer over the sterilisers. He walked in quietly and stood there watching me for a moment, and then he said with sudden urgency: 'For heaven's sake put that mop down and come into the surgeons' room. I want to talk to you.'

I looked up and saw his face, and it was enough. 'Yes, sir,' I said. The last grains of sand ran down as I switched off. 'Right away, sir.'

In the surgeons' room he closed the door and turned the key. 'There. Perhaps I can *now* have you to myself for five minutes.'

'Matron'll sack me if she finds me locked in here with a consultant!' I protested. 'It's the one thing that's not on. It rates instant dismissal.'

'Do you care?'

'Not much,' I said.

He stood two yards away from me and held out a sheet of paper, and his voice was unsteady. 'Genevieve sent this. She said she promised it to a Nurse Lake. Would that be you?'

It was one of those delightful children's drawings. A nurse with a cap and apron, and a lilac-chalked dress. She had enormous eyes with lashes sticking out all round, and a superb pair of legs. Underneath was written: *Nurse A. Lake, by G. Dell. P.S. Daddy did the legs.*

'Daddy flattered me,' I said. I wanted to cry, and that was absurd.

'I don't think he did.' He still kept his distance. 'Annabel, I couldn't get in touch. I had to leave you to sort things out with Fitzgibbon.'

'But I told you in my note,' I said. 'And you didn't answer it, so I thought—'

'What note?'

'You said I was to write to you, as part of my homework. And I did. But you didn't answer.'

He was puzzled. 'I got a practice piece, yes. Not a note.'

I thought of the way I'd poured my heart out, and wondered how he could possibly call it a 'practice piece'. 'What did it say?'

'Oh, let's think. I know. "Sister Pleydell is married; Staff Beddoes is not." Words to that effect.'

That had been on the next page, at the back of my dietetics notebook. I hadn't made an idiot of myself after all. I hadn't been snubbed, and everything was all right. 'I'm a perfect fool,' I said. 'I must have torn out the wrong sheet.'

'What did you think you'd sent?'

'It doesn't matter now,' I said. 'It wasn't important. Forget it.'

He opened his arms then and I went to him at once. We didn't even kiss. It was enough, for a minute or two, to be close. Then Simon drew in a great shuddering breath and pushed me away, but he kept one hand in his. 'Let's be quite sure, Abby,' he said. He fumbled in his pocket again. 'I'm ashamed to say that I stole this. I took it when you weren't in a position to stop me.' It was a well dog-eared fold of lined paper.

'What is it?'

He unfolded it. 'It was on the desk in Casualty, the night you were attacked. And you'd written it so beautifully.'

It said: *All my love to Simon.*

'I'd copied it from the fly-leaf of one of the books!'

'I know, my love. Point is, did you mean it? *Do* you mean it? I've got to know.'

I let out my breath at last. 'Yes, Simon.'

Things happened rather fast then. When I next took note of my surroundings I was sitting on Simon's lap in the big leather armchair without my cap. Suddenly it was all unthinkable. 'You can't *do* this!' I said. 'Simon, you're a consultant. You can't sit here with a third-year on your lap. What Matron would say if she knew—'

He murmured something about Matron that didn't sound in the least complimentary, and then he said: 'Abby, you *are* going to marry me, aren't you?'

I stroked down the unruly tuft of hair at the back of his head and loved it. 'You haven't exactly asked me to.'

'I'm asking you now. Abby, will you?' He put his warm cheek against mine. 'Please.'

'That's my line,' I told him shakily. 'I'm the one who says "please", you know.'

'Abby—'

'Oh, Simon! Yes, please. But not until I've taken the State final.'

'When does it begin?'

'Day after tomorrow.'

He smiled. 'Very well. Whenever you say, darling, as long as you say "yes".'

'I do,' I told him. 'And I shan't change my mind.'

He sighed. 'And I was so sure it would be Fitzgibbon, all the time I was away.'

'So was I, Simon, at one time. What odd mistakes people make. I don't know now what he had for me. I never really knew him until last week.' Then I heard footsteps. 'Simon! There's Staff Beddoes. Let me unlock the door, quickly.'

'Certainly not. Not until you've kissed me again.'

'But I shall—' There was no finishing that. And when we did walk out Staff Beddoes only looked amused, and said that she'd seen it coming, and now would I please get on with setting for that glioma of Mr Harriman's?

Two splendid things happened next day. First thing after breakfast Miss Black told me that I was through the surgery re-take with 87 per cent. Five minutes later I found a thick letter from Simon in my pigeonhole. He must have spent half the night writing it. It was pretty repetitive, but that didn't matter. It seemed to me that it was the first real love-letter I'd ever had in my life. He said, too, that he'd 'asked Genevieve's consent' and that she heartily approved. *You should have seen her face,* he wrote. *And unlike most stepdaughters she does NOT want to call you something other than 'Mummy'. I'm sure that will tell you a great deal, because you are wise and kind, and won't expect me to elaborate on the less happy parts of our past. They are wiped out now: as my wife and Genevieve's Mummy you will be fulfilling the true function of a nurse—to heal. And though we don't much mind whether you actually pass your State or not, we both send you all our good wishes.* It went back to being repetitious after that, and I folded it small and put it in my watch-pocket over my heart.

I told Triss and Molly just before we went in to begin the State next day in the cleared recreation room. And they must have told the others pretty quickly, because everyone except Fletcher kept turning round to grin at me and make thumbs-up signs before we were told to settle down. Even B. J. Williams, and she went through clapping motions too, until Miss Black said: 'Quiet, every-body! Be ready to turn over your papers when I tell you.'

A moment later I was reading over the surgery questions. The fourth—and it carried 40 per cent of the marks—was: *Describe in detail the surgical treatment, and nursing preparation and after care, in a case of calculus in the common bile duct.*

I smiled blissfully at Miss Black and the other invigilators, and then closed my eyes and watched Simon's hands moving. I listened to his voice too. After a while I sat up, took up the new broad-nibbed pen, and wrote it all down in the best italic script I could manage.

I was proud of it when I had finished, but it was nothing compared with the letter I meant to write to Simon when I got to my room. It was nice to think that my first real letter to him wasn't going to be in illegible scribble, because I wanted him to be able to read every word. And because I hoped he would keep it, the way he'd kept my first practice-piece. There were some things we could talk about, things like the house, and Mrs Grocock, but there were others I could only write, in my very best handwriting, once and for ever.

A very special gift for Mother's Day

You love Mills & Boon romances. Your mother will love this attractive Mother's Day gift pack. First time in paperback, four superb romances by leading authors. A very special gift for Mother's Day.

United Kingdom £4.40   On sale from 24th Feb 1984

A Grand Illusion
Maura McGiveny

Sensual Encounter
Carole Mortimer

Desire in the Desert
Mary Lyons

Aquamarine
Madeleine Ker

Look for this gift pack where you buy Mills & Boon romances.

4 BOOKS FREE
Enjoy a Wonderful World of Romance…

Passionate and intriguing, sensual and exciting. A top quality selection of four Mills & Boon titles written by leading authors of Romantic fiction can be delivered direct to your door absolutely FREE!

Try these Four Free books as your introduction to Mills & Boon Reader Service. You can be among the thousands of women who enjoy six brand new Romances every month PLUS a whole range of special benefits.

- Personal membership card.
- Free monthly newsletter packed with recipes, competitions, exclusive book offers and a monthly guide to the stars.
- Plus extra bargain offers and big cash savings.

There is no commitment whatsoever, no hidden extra charges and your first parcel of four books is absolutely FREE!

Why not send for more details now? Simply complete and send the coupon to MILLS & BOON READER SERVICE, P.O. BOX 236, THORNTON ROAD, CROYDON, SURREY, CR9 3RU, ENGLAND. OR why not telephone us on 01-684 2141 and we will send you details about the Mills & Boon Reader Service Subscription Scheme — you'll soon be able to join us in a wonderful world of Romance.

Please note:– **READERS IN SOUTH AFRICA write to Mills & Boon Ltd., Postbag X3010, Randburg 2125, S. Africa.**

Please send me details of the Mills & Boon Reader Service Subscription Scheme.

NAME (Mrs/Miss) _____ EP6

ADDRESS _____

_____

COUNTY/COUNTRY _____

POSTCODE _____

BLOCK LETTERS PLEASE